GANGLAND

A Real Chicago Love Story

A NOVEL BY

LEO SULLIVAN
PORSCHA STERLING

This SULLIVAN PRODUCTIONS, LLC book is being published by

Leo Sullivan Presents
P.O. Box 924043
Norcross, GA 30010

eISBN: 978-1-946789-26-6

Cover Designer: Marion Designs

JOIN OUR MAILING LIST!

Join our mailing list to get a notification when Leo Sullivan Presents has another release.

Text LEOSULLIVAN to 22828 to join!

To submit a manuscript for our review, email us.

SYNOPSIS

At 17-years-old, Star can't wait to graduate so that she can make it out the Southside. With dreams of making it big, she is already on the right track to a new life after building a following by doing make-up tutorials and posting sexy photos of herself on her Instagram page. Though a good girl, she's infatuated with the violent and merciless street king, Polo, the head of the city's most notorious gang. She wants nothing more than to help him drop his current girl so that she can be the woman in his life. But Star gets more than she bargained for when a series of events lead her to not only be Polo's main chick but forces her to be the leader of the female counterpart to his gang.

Tragedy strikes when Star's own dope fiend of a mother robs Polo's trap house and the act sends Mink, Polo's baby brother, and Kato, Polo's right-hand man, blasting right through Star's front door. When the night ends with Kato shot and Mink murdered at Star's hands, Polo demands to know who is responsible for killing his brother but she quickly covers her own tracks to save herself from his wrath.

Unfortunately, Star doesn't know there is a witness to her crime. Kato, who she thought she'd killed is actually alive and in a coma fighting for his life. When he suddenly awakes, Star is afraid that her fate will be sealed as soon as he tells how Mink really died. However,

Kato is not the same man that he was before and things between the two quickly begin to change. When sparks fly and Star feels she's found true love in the one man she thought she hated more than anyone on Earth, will the real truth of her lies come to light and ruin it all?

This is the first part of a series written not for the faint at heart. Brace yourselves for a story of love, loyalty and survival on Chicago's Southside.

WARNING

This book contains bad language, violence and some explicit sex scenes. This is a work of fiction. Names, characters, business, events and incidents are the products of the author's imagination. Any resemblance to actual persons, living or dead, or actual events is purely coincidental.

This is a cautionary tale. In no way do the authors promote or condone acts of violence, rape, gang activity or any criminal activity that may be illustrated within this novel.

PROLOGUE

THERE ARE CONSEQUENCES TO FALLING FOR A THUG. IT'S NOT ALL glitz, glamor, fast cars, and stunting on the city while standing next to a man who is both respected and feared just as much as he's loved... but no one ever talks about that. No one ever talks about the not so good side of being in love with a man who has made a name in the streets based off his aggression, carelessness, and propensity to be violent. No one speaks about the emotional toll that comes with loving a man like that to the point that you may be the one to turn his heart warm after years of it being so cold.

There is a dark side that many don't see, because very few have the courage to share the tale of what it's *really* like to be in love with a man who was never taught to love in the first place. It's not all good, and it's not all full of spontaneous fun. And no one knew this fact better than Star, who had not only fallen in love with one thug but *two*.

"Why you lookin' at me like that? Is it the scar?"

Star cut her eyes away from Kato's face and looked down at her trembling hands. The man she loved with her whole heart was sitting right in front of her, and she was holding a secret so terrible that simply thinking about it made her stomach twist up into painful knots. Today was the day that Kato would be released from the hospital. It should have been a happy day, something worthy of a celebration, but with every day that passed, Kato came closer and closer to a full recovery, and Star was hit with the realization that once he remembered the day that he'd gotten the ugly scar on the side of his face and who was *actually* responsible for putting it there, her life would be over. There was no way he would allow her to take another breath once he found out the truth.

"It's not the scar," she assured him, forcing out a smile.

Although a nice gesture, her lips were tense around the edges, and even Kato could see that it was strained. Stepping forward, she ran her finger over the scar on the side of his face. It was a miracle that after such a life-threatening injury to the head, this was all the evidence left behind. Even with it, Kato's sexiness wasn't any less. His strength showed in his face, even in his weakest moments. And then there were those peculiar green eyes...

Star had to blink a few times and then glance away to keep her mind from delving into her secret forbidden fantasies and return to the present.

"I'm just happy that you finally get to leave. You recovered so fast after coming out of the coma..."

That I put you in, she completed to herself.

Her eyes lowered in shame, and she swallowed hard, hoping her guilt didn't show in her face. She was the one who had held the gun and fired the bullet that nearly killed him and placed him into a coma that stole a large part of his memory. Back then, she hated him —she had *wanted* him to die—but this was not the same Kato from before.

During the past few weeks that she'd spent by his bedside, nursing him into the person he was today, her feelings had changed. Their moments together moved her from repulsion to admiration of the man he was, and now she was helplessly in love. She didn't want to admit it, but she couldn't see her life without him... These days, he was nearly the only thing that made her life worth living.

However, he was remembering more and more about his past every day. What would happen when he realized that she had almost killed him—had actually *tried* and was in fact disappointed after finding out that she'd failed? Would the killer in him return to the surface? Would he turn the gun on her and end her life instead?

"I don't wanna talk about that shit anymore," Kato said, dismissing her with a slight wave of his hand. "I'm just ready to get back to doing what I do. This laying in the bed shit ain't for me."

Star paused, looking away while collecting her thoughts, and he watched her intensely, reading her body language. He knew her well enough to know that something was off, but he wasn't exactly sure about what it was. Looking at her arms, he noted the ill-covered bruises on her skin and wanted to ask her about them, but he immediately shook the thought away, knowing that it wasn't his place. Star was Polo's girl, and Polo was not only his best friend, but he was the leader of the Gangster Disciples, the gang he'd pledged his life and loyalty to.

Kato's feelings were already too much involved, and he had to be careful not to cross the line with Star any more than he already had. Although he hadn't asked her directly, he was suspicious that Polo was responsible for the markings he'd seen on her body as well as her sudden change from the confident, outspoken, and fiery woman that she'd been into the quiet, nearly silent, timid, and almost childlike person she was now. Her light used to shine so bright that you could pick up on her aura about a mile away. Now, she was only a shell of herself, so cautious about her actions, so careful about her words, and so apologetic about the simplest things. He didn't like it, and he wanted to bring the gangsta back out of her, but she wasn't his, and he couldn't interfere... at least not in the way he wished.

Sighing, he made a move to stand to his feet and staggered slightly, losing his balance. In a flash, Star was on him, wrapping her arms around his waist to steady him.

His body tensed. Just the feel of her touch froze the blood in his veins.

Shit... nigga, you're trippin', he chastised himself. His reaction to her was incredulous even to him; he'd never responded this way to any woman.

"You should let me help you," she said, but he nudged her gently back, shaking his head.

"Not necessary. I'm a little shaky, but I got this. I'm a muthafuckin'

G, remember?" he asked with a teasing half-smile to put her at ease after seeing her flinch from being pushed away.

Star looked into his face and felt her cheeks start to flame, but she did as he asked and took a few steps back to give him some room. Kato took his time collecting himself, and she bit down on her bottom lip as she watched, noting the way that his muscular physique showed, even through his clothes. Even being bedridden for so long didn't take away from his muscular frame. He was still a beast inside and out, but much calmer than before... much easier to love.

Kato stood tall, allowing his massive figure to hover above her, and she dropped her eyes. Big mistake. The gray sweatpants he wore taunted her by showing off a large bulge that set her sexual desire on fire. She blinked and looked away, attempting to quiet the beating of her heart. If only he knew how many nights she'd gone to bed lying next to Polo but fantasizing about him instead. And if Polo had ever found out about her late-night thoughts, it would have been her lying up in the hospital bed instead.

"Aye," Kato said, calling out to her. "Look at me."

When she didn't respond, he reached out and placed his fingers lightly under her chin, pulling her eyes up until they met his. She sucked in a breath, and her heart skipped two beats. It was like staring into the eyes of the one man that God had created specifically for her. How cruel that fate would have it that they could never be?

"You should know by now that you can tell me anything. What's wrong?" he asked, ignoring the voice in his mind that told him to let this subject go. It wasn't right... She wasn't his. But who could ignore the urgings of the heart? He couldn't, and neither could she.

Yes, something is very wrong, Star thought. *I'm in love with you, but if Polo finds out, he'll kill me. And once you remember that I'm the one who shot you and killed his little brother, you'll do the job for him.*

Before she could say a word, the door behind them opened, making Star nearly jump out of her skin. Turning, she found herself staring right into Polo's hardened face, and her honey brown complexion seemed to pale.

Kato's eyes narrowed as he noted the sudden change in her. He lingered on her face for a few seconds longer before turning his attention to his friend. His expression was blank but his mind was reeling with alarming thoughts. Something wasn't right. Star was visibly afraid, nervous even, and her hands were trembling even more than before. These were all signs that confirmed Kato's suspicions that she was being abused, and he was certain that it was Polo who was behind it. But there wasn't a damn thing he could do.

"Nigga, you look brand new!" Polo said, walking into the room.

He swaggered with the poise of a king, showing off a smile wide enough to display every single one of his gold-plated teeth. Seeing Kato standing healthy and tall made his day. It was hard being a street king without your most cherished soldier standing by your side. He'd always appreciated having Kato on his team, but now more than ever, he knew the true value of his presence.

On the contrary, Kato stood silent, giving Polo only a simple nod. His eyes were no longer on Star, and he had increased the distance between them, but Polo was smart enough to know that he'd interrupted something by his presence. What, he didn't exactly know, but the tension in the air was palpable. Rolling his eyes from Kato's face in order to pierce them through Star, Polo scowled at her as she stood with her head bent to the floor.

"The fuck goin' on with you?" He posed this question to her in a much different tone than the congenial one he'd used for Kato. These days, his tone was much more aggressive than kind, to the point that she could barely remember the days when it was any other way.

"Nothing, I—"

"Then move your fuckin' feet and go grab his bags, bitch! My nigga finally gettin' to come home."

Kato bit down on his tongue to stop himself from speaking and instead ran his hand over his mouth as he watched Star jump to do as she was asked. Plenty of times in the past he'd referred to women as 'bitches', even called Star one a few times, but something about Polo saying it now got under his skin. Still, he forced himself to keep quiet, clamping down so hard on his tongue that he could taste his own blood.

Replacing his sneer with a friendly grin, Polo walked over and smacked hands with Kato, happy to see his right-hand man on his feet again. It had been a long journey, but he was more than ready to have him back. Kato was his enforcer, the one nigga in the squad that was responsible for carrying out his orders and providing punishment to those who didn't obey. Now that he was back, Polo could properly get back to being at the top of his game. There was only one thing that he needed to address before he could get started with business as usual.

"What they say about your memory?" he asked Kato, cocking his head to the side.

Staring at him from the corner of her eyes, Star shuddered, thinking about how much he reminded her of a snake as he posed the question. It was hard to think about how obsessed she'd been with Polo at one time, because these days, she could barely stand the sight of him.

"I ain't tryin' to rush you or no shit like that, but the sooner you can tell me your side of what went down the night my brother was killed, the sooner I can put my mind at ease."

Lifting one brow, Polo peeked over his shoulder at Star and saw the way that her breath seemed to stall as she waited for Kato's response. She was on edge, the same way that she always was whenever he asked Kato about that night, which led him to believe that she wasn't being as truthful about it as she pretended to be. Kato picked up on her uneasiness as well, but he had other suspicions about why Star seemed fearful in Polo's presence.

"In no time, I'll be back on point, fam. Best believe, once I remember all the details, you'll be the first nigga to know, bruh."

Satisfied with that response, Polo pensively licked his lips and then nodded his head slowly. They said to keep your friends close but your enemies closer, and that was exactly what he was doing when it came to Star. Yeah, she was sexy as fuck and the perfect trophy to have by his side—and as the leader of the Black Gangstress, Star really had no choice but to belong to him being that he ran the Gangster Disciples. But he had other much darker and malicious reasons for keeping her so close. He couldn't be sure, but he knew that she was involved in his brother's murder somehow, and as soon as he could prove what he suspected to be true, he would have his revenge on her and everyone else responsible.

"That's what's up," Polo replied, still staring at Star as she struggled with Kato's duffle bags. "Bitch, hurry the fuck up! Movin' like you got a stick up yo' fuckin' ass. We ain't tryin' to be here all day."

Seemingly unbothered by his disrespect, Star continued to fuss with the bags. At one point in her life, she would have knocked the teeth out of someone's mouth for addressing her in that way, but not these days. Polo called her 'bitch' so much that in the rare times that he actually said her name, it didn't even sound right coming from his lips.

Watching her reaction, or lack of one rather, was disturbing to Kato, who could barely recognize the woman Star had become. It agitated him in the worst way, and he knew that he had to make a move to distance himself from this situation quickly, before shit turned sour. He was used to the mouthy, aggressive woman that Star had been when they'd first met. Every now and then when they were alone, he would get a glimpse of the fiery spirited woman she used to be, but for the most part, that person was long gone, thanks to Polo. The last thing Kato could do was sit around and watch him continue to reduce her to shit.

Sniffing, Kato nudged his nose slightly before walking over and grabbing the bags from Star and placing them on his shoulders.

"I got this shit," he said in a tone that had an edge of anger in it. "I'll meet y'all outside."

Star snatched her head up to look at him, picking up on the steel in his voice and mistakenly thinking that it was meant for her. It wasn't. Polo was pissing him off, and he had to get out of the room as fast as possible before things took a turn that he wasn't prepared for. For once in his life, Kato was able to use a bit of self-control, but he couldn't continue to be tested. He made his exit in a rush, slamming the door behind him and leaving both Polo and Star behind.

Silence loomed in his absence, but the tension in the air was so thick that Star could barely breathe. She was terrified of being alone with Polo. As time passed, his cruel nature seemed to only magnify to bigger proportions. He was nothing like the man she'd once fantasized about being with. He was a monster, her torturer. If she could see a way to get away from him without fearing that he'd one day show up and snatch the breath from her body, she would. But she was trapped. In this city, Polo was king, and she was forced to be his queen.

"Kato's memory will be back soon... that's some good shit, huh?" he said in a tone that was almost taunting.

She lifted her head to look into his eyes, and she could see him searching through her, trying to read her so that he could pick up on her deepest thoughts. Forcing herself to smile, she nodded her head and pushed out a lie through her teeth.

"Yes, it is."

Walking over to her, Polo grabbed her roughly by her throat, and she gasped out a breath, her eyes widening in horror. But before she could react, he lowered his head and silenced the scream rising from her throat with his lips, kissing her so deeply that it stung once he finally pulled away. It was like the kiss of death.

This is crazy, were her thoughts as she went through the motions of a passionate embrace.

Truthfully, 'crazy' was an understatement. At one point, she'd laid in bed at night thinking about how great it would be to be Polo's woman. Being with him came with the type of status that her young mind could only dream of. He was the king of Chi-city, and she was his ride or die, which meant that, together, they were the hood's most powerful couple. What wasn't to like about that?

But being with Polo was nothing like a fairytale, and she felt less like a princess and more like a slave. There was a thin line between love and hate, and it took no time at all for her emotions to change. There was no one in the world that she detested more than she did him. It was almost as if every emotion she had once felt for Kato had been transferred to Polo and vice versa.

If she could just go back to the day when things first started falling in line to make her his girl, she would make drastic changes to ensure that they'd never met. But there was no point in crying over the past or being sad about things that she couldn't change. She alone had made the decision to be with the most feared man in the Midwest. Her body belonged to Polo although her heart yearned for Kato, and there was nothing anyone could do about it.

CHAPTER 1

"To dream of a life without crime, without lost and without suffering, is a privilege for a child growing up on the Southside of Chicago."

WHILE SHE SLEPT, STAR DREAMED OF HER GRADUATION... THE DAY that she would finally walk across the stage. It felt so real she could almost feel the soft fibers of her graduation gown flowing against her thick thighs as she strutted toward the stage with her head lifted high, gliding across the freshly-waxed gym floor in stiletto heels so high she felt she was walking on stilts. This was the day that she'd worked so hard toward.

Being the oldest of her mother's children and growing up in a family where women fought for baby daddies instead of diplomas, Star was doing something unheard of before. Really, she wasn't even sure her mother and grandmother valued education, because they'd never pressed the importance of it upon her. The hardships of everyday life forced them to think of more tangible things: food, rent, and in her mother's case, crack cocaine. Not once had they asked her whether her homework was done or what grade she'd received on a test, but it was fine because she didn't need that type of motivation to get the job done. She had dreams of being like Oprah—a woman who was able to push past the dead-end road that being poor in a place like Chicago placed her on and rose up to levels that everyone could only dream of reaching. Through hard work and dedication to that cause, she just knew she could make it.

So she made her plans, wrote them down on paper to make them as visible to her eyes as they were in her heart, and kept them hidden in her nightstand drawer so that no one would laugh at her for having high hopes. She glanced at that paper every morning before she started her day, using it as a constant reminder that she was better than what she saw around her.

With a slick ass mouth, fearless attitude, and confrontational personality that appeared more aggressive and bolder than how she really felt on the inside, at first glance, Star seemed to be a typical hood chick, but being typical didn't fit the vision that she'd created for herself. She wanted to live life like Beyoncé and jet set all around the world with her own sexy ass version of Jay Z; her man had to be both gentleman and thug. As far as kids, Star didn't really want them, but if it came down to it, she'd pop out a baby or two. With all the money, fame, and prestige that the world had to offer, she was certain that a nanny would come with all that so that she wouldn't falter on building her career and dreams.

With graduation around the corner and Northwestern University, her college of choice, offering her a full ride scholarship, she could almost see the finish line she'd been working all her life toward. She was only weeks out from making it out of the Chicago Southside, and once she did that, no one could stop her from achieving more. Keeping her desires secret from everyone but her little sister, Ebony, was hard, but she didn't want to deal with anyone talking noise. It was already bad enough that she had to pretend like she didn't know shit in order to keep from being looked at as an outcast or picked on. The last thing she needed was some big mouth, hatin' ass female to tell her that she was stupid for aiming for the stars when she was living in the slums— especially now when she was so close to achieving everything on her list.

All she had to do was survive the Southside.

. . .

THE SOUND of a door slamming so hard that the walls shook suddenly pulled Star from out of a deep sleep, and she sat straight up in the bed, holding her breath, and straining her ears to listen. The murmur of hushed voices trailed down the hallway, concurrent with the heavy shuffling of feet. A splinter of light passed under her room door, and she hurriedly rushed to grab the small gun that she kept in her night-stand for protection. She was a good girl, but she was brave and had the heart of a gangsta. If it came down to protecting her family, she kept a pistol on her and wouldn't think twice about using it.

"We got they ass! We got they ass! I told you they had that shit stashed back there in the bushes behind the house!"

The victorious chant came from the lips of her mother, Roxy, so Star relaxed only slightly, but then she heard the voice of a man and thought twice, deciding to hold the gun a little while longer.

"Them niggas ain't gon' know what hit 'em," the man bragged before a long pause. "Wait... you think they saw us?"

"Nigga, did *you* see *them*?" There was a mumbled 'uh-uh' before Roxy continued. "Well then, they ain't see you!"

Star rolled her eyes at that. A crack-head's reasoning.

"All the shit we got gon' have us set for life!"

Roxy's high-pitched voice sent a timorous shiver down Star's spine, and she was overcome with dread. She didn't know what exactly was going on, but one thing was for certain: her mama always had some shit going on, and it was never good. Sitting as still as a statue, she continued to listen to them speak.

"Where dat pipe at, nigga?" Roxy asked right outside her door. "You talk too damn much with dat squeaky ass voice. I'm tryna get high!"

Grasping the gun tightly in her hand, her curiosity got the best of her, and Star began to get up to peek out of the door. Suddenly, there was a loud noise that nearly made her jump out of her skin. It took a moment for her alarm to fade, but when it did, she realized that the brand-new iPhone she'd saved up all summer to buy had fallen off her bed and landed face down on the wood floor. She nearly had a fit as she snatched it up and then ran over to turn on the room light so that she could assess the damage.

Roaches scattered away from a half-eaten piece of pizza that she'd left on her dresser, but she was so focused on her phone that she didn't even flinch. Seeing the screen severely scratched made her heart drop to her feet. For many, a broken phone wasn't anything. But to a teenage girl who used the freedom of the internet to escape, it was *everything*. How would she stay up on all the latest gossip now?

Outside her door, she could still hear her mother and the mystery man speaking to each other, but her attention was elsewhere. Checking Instagram, the first picture to pop up on the screen was of Polo, her crush and the leader of the Gangster Disciples, also known as the Disciples or Black Gangstas, Chicago's most notorious gang. And by his side was of course his bitch... Tonya.

To be completely honest, Star couldn't stand her, but she knew that she was simply hating because of the man she was with, though she'd never admit it. Tonya was drop-dead gorgeous with a curvy body, slim waist, pretty face, and a plump ass. She and Polo always wore the finest gear. They were relationship goals for sure.

Tonya and Polo were hood legends. Polo had nearly half a million followers on the 'Gram, and so did Tonya. What made them so dope was that Tonya was the female leader of the notorious Chicago Black Gangstress, the female counterpart to the Disciples. Together, they made an infamous tandem; they were respected by most and feared by many. They were the street version of Bonnie and Clyde, only much worse.

Chicago was the murder capital of the nation with most of them occurring right in Englewood, where Star had been born and raised, and the majority of the murders directly related to the Gangsta Disciples organization, with Polo sitting at the helm. The original leader of the gang was Larry Hoover, but the oldest living O.G. at this time was Jimmy Johnson, who was on death row for a slew of murders with his execution imminent, although he consistently proclaimed his innocence. Under his word, Polo ran the city with an ironclad fist. The entire organization was huge, with over two hundred thousand strong, and it operated like a governmental system, with governors, dons, chief enforcers, chief advisers, and foot soldiers at the bottom. Polo was a governor, and he only took his orders from the boss of all bosses, Jimmy Johnson.

Being that Polo was often seen at a trap house known as 'The Spot' on 63rd Street, the same block where Star lived with her grandmother, she'd been watching him and fantasizing about everything they could be for a minute. The thrill of grabbing the attention of someone so feared and respected was everything she thought she wanted. She would sit outside for hours watching him make his moves and fantasizing that she was the woman he went home to at night. If an opportunity arose where she was able to walk by him, making sure to put an extra swish in her ass, she took it every time. Though she was a thick girl and was often told by Roxy that she could stand to lose a couple pounds, the look in Polo's eyes said otherwise. She lived for those moments. The little bit of attention he gave her did miracles for her self-esteem.

Turning the light back off, Star returned to her bed and continued to stare at the glow of the phone in the dark. There was an ugly spiderweb crack in the left-hand corner of her screen, thanks to the fall.

"Fuck!" she cursed, reaching toward the nightstand to return the gun to the drawer. Then she glanced toward her closed door and remembered the man she'd heard speaking with Roxy and switched gears, tucking it under the covers instead.

Shaking her head in distress, Star decided to check her own Instagram page, noticing that she had about eighteen thousand followers, just shy of her goal of twenty thousand. She'd been posting pictures wearing various bathing suits with her hair and makeup done flawlessly, to build up her followers, and it was finally starting to pay off. You would never know that her family was on Section 8 and that most of her clothes were not designer but had come from either Wal-Mart or a low-budget department store.

"Star? Star, is that you, girl?" her mama called out. She could hear feet shuffling around in the hallway and gritted her teeth. They were loud as hell and would definitely wake her grandmother up if they didn't hush.

Here she go with this bullshit.

Biting down on her bottom lip, Star started not to say a word. It was bad enough that she had to sleep with a gun by her side just because she had a crack fiend for a mama who was always bringing bullshit to their front door. Every day, Star either had to deal with getting robbed by her own mama or fending off the niggas she'd bring around who would come to see her but then end up sneaking around the house, trying to pull Star or her little sister's panties down. *And these were grown ass men!* No matter how many times Star mentioned, Roxy still didn't give a damn.

"Star!"

"Yes, Mama?" she said with an irritated tone, finally answering only because she didn't want her granny to be disturbed.

Her grandmother, Geraldine, had cancer, and her sickness sometimes made her mean as a snake. No one could complain. They all were living in her house, as Geraldine reminded them fairly often. As Star waited for her mama to answer, she looked down at the cracked screen on her phone once more. The ambient glow on the iPhone read 3:43 a.m. What the hell was Roxy up to this damn early in the morning?

Pushing that thought from her mind, Star couldn't resist going back to Instagram to look at the picture of Polo. *God, he was so fiiiine!*

She couldn't help but let out a goofy love-struck smile as she watched a video of him at the gym working out, body tatted, all sweaty, and sexy as fuck! His swag was impeccable. Polo was a savage through and through, and that thug appeal had her mesmerized. Her little young heart had created its own fantasy of what it was like to be with a man as supreme as this, and she begged God every day for just a chance to show Polo that she was the one he was looking for.

The same dumb smile was still plastered on Star's face when Roxy snatched her door open and walked right into her room. A dim glow of light spilled inside as two silhouettes stood looking down at her—her mama and her junkie friend.

Roxy had a crack pipe in one hand; it was smoldering, still lit, with a ball of ardent red fire luminous from the top. The smell of crack smoke hit Star heavy in her face, causing her to frown in disgust. Roxy cut the light on in a flash, and Star glared at the man standing before her, looking her over with a lusty stare. He had beady eyes and sported an old school afro, short crop. Though old as hell, he was staring with greed at Star's breasts under the thin lace nighty that she was wearing.

Sick muthafucka, she thought, curling her top lip.

"Y'all need to get out of here so I can sleep!" she shouted and pulled the covers up to her chin, shielding herself from the nasty man who was now ogling her with a sneaky smile on his face. Roxy was so high, she had no idea what was happening around her. Either that or she simply didn't care.

"Heffa, you ain't sleep. I saw that phone in your hand! Hurry and get your fat ass up. I need you to keep this!"

Roxy rushed over and shoved a big ass dirty garbage bag at Star, allowing dirt and grit to fall in her bed. Frowning, she looked up at her mother and saw as her eyes rolled around in her head. A sheen of perspiration gleamed on Roxy's forehead while smoke rose from her mouth to the ceiling, fumigating Star's entire room. But it was the unwashed stench from her body that really turned her nose. She pinched it closed with one hand and used the other to wave Roxy and her funk away.

"Mama, get out! I gotta go to school in the morning. Every time you get high, you come in here messing with me. Damn!"

Star kicked at the sheets, making a pack of blunts and a bag of Loud she'd been smoking from, fall onto the floor. The man hopped back, startled; his eyes were big as saucers as a ball of sweat cascaded down his forehead. He was looking at Star's naked thigh that was now partially exposed. Panic gripped Star's heart. She had seen that look in a man's eyes before.

"Mama, get outta here with all that noise! You know Granny tryna sleep. And what the hell is this?" she yelled, holding the trash bag up in the air. Her face was still balled up as she wrinkled her nose further. The stench coming from her Roxy's body was overwhelming.

Through a cloud of smoke, Roxy answered with a shrug. "It's money, lots of money. We robbed Polo's crew. Caught them niggas slippin'." She did some sort of jerky motion and looked at the floor like she had lost something.

"You did whaaat?"

Star sat up straight in the bed, wide-awake, with her heart

pounding in her chest like a bass drum. There was no way she could have heard this crazy ass woman right.

"Why you trippin'?" Roxy chirped, frowning down at Star like she was being ungrateful. "With you here, they would never suspect us. You told me you needed money for makeup and shit. Well, now you got it."

That said, Roxy stared at her daughter expectantly as if waiting for her praises to be sung. Star's mouth fell wide open. Sheer terror gripped her soul.

"You're wrong," she whispered, her eyes scanning the wall behind her mother as she thought things through. "If they find out what you've done, not even I can protect you."

At seventeen-years-old, Star was a Black Gangstress by way of force and not by choice. Being a Gangstress meant that she was able to roll with some of the baddest, notorious bitches in the Midwest and she was also associated with the Disciples; providing her a kind of elitism like no other in the hood. She was nearly untouchable and 'unfuck-withable', which was the perfect cover to move through her part of the Southside without worrying about whether or not she'd make it home each day. Finally, she had a crew standing behind her if her slick ass mouth wrote a check that her ass wasn't ready to cash but this stunt that Roxy pulled? If she was found out, there was nothing Star could do.

In Roxy's world, where the fantasies of a junkie reigned supreme, she'd outsmarted one of the most feared gangstas and was already cele-brating the victory. Sucking from the crack pipe in her hand, also known as the Devil's Dick, Roxy couldn't be in a happier state. But Star knew how Polo and his crew moved. You didn't see them coming until they were there and by then, it was already too late.

Standing, Star padded over to her bedroom window and then peered out into the darkness. Her hands were shaking so badly that you could hear the rattling of the plastic garbage bag that she was still holding. Thankfully, there was nothing outside moving, just obscure blackness and gray smog. She took a deep breath and tried to relax but still couldn't.

Just as she was about to turn away from the window, a blue Dodge

Charger suddenly pulled up, its headlights slicing through the night before coming to a stop right in front of her building. She sucked in a breath and watched it, not moving a muscle. The Charger looked familiar to her as it sat idly and ominous in the night. Nothing good would come from this.

Pulling away from the window with her mind racing and thoughts percolating, Star looked between Roxy and the man in her room. They were oblivious to everything around them and were fussing over the crack pipe. If she wasn't scared to death, the sight might have been comical. Still shivering, Star eased her hand inside the large trash bag and peeked down to see what was inside. There had to be at least a hundred grand or more in cash! Gasping, she dropped the bag to the floor and backed away like it was on fire.

"Mama, you need to tell me how you got this money." Her voice screeched with fear and her instincts kept telling her that something terrible was about to happen. She couldn't be more right. Apparently, Roxy hadn't gotten the memo.

"It was easy! Lemme tell you," Roxy began, smiling and clapping her hands together as she prepared to tell her daughter the story of how she'd saved the day. They would have enough money to live high on the hog for the rest of their days, in her mind. She'd be able to buy all the dope that she could dream of, and Star could cash out on enough of that makeup shit she'd been begging for to paint her entire body with Rihanna's Fenty Body Glitter for life.

"So I went and bought a dime rock from Polo's little brother, Mink, and me and Steve went out back to smoke it since that big ass dog he has wasn't out there. That was when we saw Mink stashing the money and drugs. Nigga didn't even see us over there watchin'—"

Star nearly choked on her own tongue as her legs went wobbly. She grabbed Roxy by her arm so hard that she flinched.

"Ouch! Girl, you hurtin' my arm," she complained and took a step back before continuing. "So I went into the backyard with Steve to get my smoke on, and like I said, out of the blue comes Mink from out his back door looking all suspicious and shit. He had these three trash bags in his hand and he pulled up that old barbecue pit then stashed it all underneath..."

Roxy paused, taking a deep breath. She stared at the pipe in her hand and began to light it as if she lost her train of thought. Then remembering she was in the middle of a story, she jumped slightly and continued.

"Oh! Where was I at? Oh yeah! So when he left, me and Steve went to investigate and this nigga done stashed all the drugs and money in there! Guns too, but we didn't take them. They was too big, but we might go back later. We got about six brick lookin' thangs of coke wrapped in plastic and tape. I stashed them in Mama's room already."

Star was petrified. She wanted to slap the shit out of Roxy and probably would have if she wasn't so focused on her own survival first.

"I think we need to get outta here," she said, feeling her stomach doing somersaults into knots as she pulled the curtains back to look out the window again.

Looking out again, she damn near pissed on herself.

Downstairs in the dense fog and looming darkness, another vehicle pulled up, some type of gray SUV, and hood niggas galore were inside piled up. The door opened to the Charger and the dome light inside showed the occupants right before they got out.

It was none other than Mink and several more of his henchmen, including Kato, his crazy ass chief enforcer. Kato was the one that Star knew for sure would shoot to kill first and ask questions later. She once saw him shoot a guy in the head for no reason other than that the guy waited too long to respond to his question while in the middle of getting pistol-whipped and robbed.

"Shit! Shit! Shit!" Star hissed in a panic. She pressed her fingers so hard against her forehead that she nearly touched her brain. She had to do something and do it quick. Mink, Kato, and a few others were marching straight for her building!

Her legs nearly buckled underneath her body, the trash bag of money slipped out of her hand as she stood at the window, terrified out of her damn mind. Her right hand, still holding the gun, quickly got sweaty. Her voice croaked when she spoke, dryly.

"Mama, listen. Do you think you can work a gun?" she asked with a feeling of despair and dread. Suddenly, it seemed like she had to pee really badly as she waited for what felt like an eternity for Roxy to answer.

Roxy pursed her lips and glared at her with a deep frown.

"Dumb ass girl, why you gon' ask me some stupid shit like that?"

"'Cause Mink, Kato, and the rest of them on they way up the stairs," Star said all in one breath. It felt like it was hard to even breathe because her heart was beating so fast.

Get yourself together, girl. You're a Gangstress, you gotta protect your family. You got this!

"Bitch, you lying!" Roxy retorted as her eyes spread wide. Her glass crack pipe dropped to the floor and broke into pieces as she dashed over to the window and looked out, followed by Steve.

"Ohh, fuck! *Fuck*! How did they find us?" Steve interjected as he jumped about six inches off the floor. "We gotta hide all the dope and money. Them Black Gangsta niggas gon' kill us," he said, full of apprehension.

High off dope, Roxy's eyes scrolled over to Steve, and she said, "Steve, if they come up in here, you gon' have to tell 'em that you stole everything, and it was an accident or something. Just claim that shit, and in return, I promise I'ma look out for your family."

She put her hand on his shoulder and he flinched, slapping it away.

"Bitch, what? I ain't tellin' them no shit like that. It was your idea to steal that shit in the first place!" Steve whined fearfully as he wrung his hands together and peered out the window.

"Right now, it ain't about what you want, Steve! Stop being a selfish asshole and just die like a man," Roxy snapped on him. "You gon' have to take this one. I can't deal with Kato's crazy ass."

"Shit, me neither! That nigga done already shot at me once because I was two dollars short that time you sent me in there with all that damn change to cop some dope," Steve responded, giving Roxy a panicked expression.

Watching the exchange, Star could barely believe that this was her life. A gang of street niggas was about to storm up in their apartment and blast everyone in sight if they didn't get their shit back and the only ones she had to depend on were the same damn crack-heads who had stolen it. She might as well spend this time to write out her own obituary because she was as good as dead.

"What y'all doin' in here making all that noise?"

Star's bedroom door opened with an eerie screech and there stood her grandmother with breathing tubes coming out of her nose and her frail hands trembling, holding on to the walker that she used for balance.

Before anyone could answer, there was a banging at the front door that caused scary ass Steve to dive straight under Star's bed. He was much too long for the small twin bed and his lanky legs peeked out from the other side. It was a disgraceful sight.

Scared beyond belief and feeling like she was surrounded by idiots, Star grabbed her gun and stashed it behind her back. She was just a little girl and wasn't ready for this life but she knew the rules of the hood. *Kill or be killed.* There was no other choice but to fight back or lay down and die like a coward. She truly felt like taking the route of the coward but she had her grandmother and little sister to think of, so she'd take her chances with fighting.

A few feet from where she stood, Roxy reached under the bed and drug Steve across the floor with both hands. His face and hair were covered with lint and debris. Star shook her head as she looked at him and realized she wouldn't be getting any assistance from Steve. When it came to fuckin' a defenseless little girl, he was ready to perform but couldn't even lift his hand to save his own life and would rather hide under the bed like a punk. What a clown.

"Come on, Steve!" Roxy said through clenched teeth, still struggling with him so ferociously that a sheen of perspiration glazed her forehead. "You *agreed* you was going to take the fall for us and work it out with Kato and 'em!"

Shocked by her words, Steve stood up quick like he had been hit with an electrical prod.

"I ain't told you no shit like that!"

"What the *hell* is going on?" Geraldine shouted with a strained voice. "Who is that knocking at this hour in the mornin' and what is that *terrible* smell?" She cut her eyes toward Roxy and scrunched up her nose in repulsion.

"Granny," Star began, licking her dry lips as she spoke carefully. "I need you to get Ebony and go hide. Some men are about to run up in here, and when they do... I may be the only one able to stop them from killing us all."

"What, child!"

Star was about to answer but her words were cut short by the sound of a heavy fist beating against the front door. Her terror was magnified as she listened to the drumming continue.

"Open this muthafuckin' door!" a voice thundered from the other side.

Star's bottom lip began to quiver but she fought to maintain her gangsta. She couldn't show fear because it would be a testament of her guilt. She had to do something and do it quickly or else they would all die tonight.

CHAPTER 2

A Few Weeks Back...

STAR WAS A BLACK GANGSTRESS BUT NOT BECAUSE SHE FOUGHT TO BE included, she never really had a choice. When people saw her rolling around with her gang, tossing up signs, flashing her colors, and running the streets, they thought this was the life that she wanted. They thought that she'd begged to be initiated because she didn't see anything else to do with her free time other than ride around and terrorize the city. They thought she needed a family, that she was a fatherless child looking for love and chose to find comfort in a gang.

They couldn't have been more wrong. The whole thing was a setup.

Growing up on the Southside, all Star knew was violence and poverty. Her earliest memories included the presence of a crack pipe; Roxy had been a fiend since before Star was even born. Somehow, she'd managed to quit the habit for the months she was pregnant but picked it right back up as soon as she pushed Star out. Like Star, Roxy once had dreams of making it big but her first hit of heroin cancelled all that and she felt hopeless to change. She named her first child 'Star' in hopes that she would live up to the name and make something of herself one day. Although regarded as a poor excuse of a mother by most, Roxy sincerely tried her best when it came to her children, she simply just didn't know how to be another type of mother than the one she was.

From the beginning, fighting came so natural to Star that it was like breathing. With thick, coarse long hair and a pretty face, many girls in the hood envied her and the easiest thing for them to hate on was her weight. Star's hips and thighs were evidence of her granny's superb cooking. Birthed in the rural countryside of Alabama, Geraldine could whip up a pot of chitterlings so juicy and hearty that you'd forget you were sucking on pig's ass and not a gourmet meal. Early on, Star earned herself a reputation in the hood for being spitfire. She was sassy, took no shit, handed out ass whoopings at the drop of a dime, and never backed down when pushed in a corner. Smart as a whip, she stayed on the honor roll but pretended like she didn't give a fuck about school so that she could fit in.

After some time, Star began to notice that almost every day when she got off the bus from school, a clique of hoes and niggas would be watching her from across the way at the trap house that Polo ran. It piqued her curiosity not knowing what they were up to, but she knew better than to ask—so when they grilled at her, she bared her teeth and grilled them right back. Her overt aggression was her defense and she hoped they would leave her alone and cast their sights on some other easy prey. The entire time, they had been plotting on her, but she was too naïve to know it.

Then something crazy happened.

Star was at the bus stop, and it was cold as hell that morning, even though it would be smoldering hot later. Chicago's weather was unpredictable. She was shivering something vicious while holding her thin bubble-coat closed. It was a coat she'd stolen out the lost and found at school, but the zipper was broken.

Chatting with Kevia, her best friend, she didn't even notice when a skinny, loud mouth, pigeon-toed, bird ass female named Brenda pulled up in a gray Benz and hopped out with two other chicks trailing behind her. They were fresh to death, rockin' royal blue coats with thick ass fox fur hoodies that cost a fortune and were only worn by the Black Gangstress crew.

"Aye, you!" Brenda called out to Star who didn't even look in her direction. She heard her talking but didn't want no drama, so she didn't make any sudden movements and prayed Brenda would just do what bird ass females like her should do, flap her wings and fly the hell away.

"I know you heard me, you fat ass girl!"

The taunt made Star's skin prickle with rage. Screw-face in place, she turned and scowled right at Brenda, fighting the urge to ball up her hands into fists. She was outnumbered, and it wasn't wise to pick a fight. The Gangstress stayed strapped.

"You talkin' to me?" Star asked, keeping her tone thick to show that she wasn't no chump. Meanwhile her eyes rolled over the face of every girl standing around, sizing them up one-by-one. Brenda had her own entourage, each girl appearing even more fearless and menacing than the next.

"Don't it fuckin' look like it?"

Not answering, Star narrowed her eyes, holding the edges of her jacket so tightly that her fingertips turned white. Brenda flipped her long, nappy weave over her shoulder and continued squawking as Star simply watched, waiting to hear what she wanted.

"I heard you was the one tryin' to fuck with my nigga and I saw your number in his phone. I ain't one to talk, so we came to holla at you—let you know what it means to fuck with a Gangstress bitch."

Frowning hard, Star shot her eyes over to Kevia, who was standing by her side, also watching with a confused expression as Brenda removed her coat and handed it over to her entourage. She had a pair of brass knuckles and pulled them on as both girls watched, wondering how the direction of their morning had changed so fast.

"Is she talkin' 'bout Kush?" Kevia whispered, looking at Star.

Kush was the neighborhood weed man, so Star definitely knew him. Her number was in his phone for business purposes only—everyone in the hood's number was in his damn phone! Who didn't get along with the weed man? Star couldn't speak for the rest of the world, but everyone around her smoked weed on the regular as a means to either cope with life or escape from it, herself included. A few times she pretended not to see him staring at her breasts in exchange for a dime bag, but other girls had done much worse in exchange for a hit. No matter the pressure he put on her for sex, Star refused to go there with him. Polo was the only one she had her eyes on.

"I ain't fuckin' with Kush," Star spoke up boldly. "Besides, if you think he's cheatin' on you, shouldn't you be checkin' your nigga instead of me? That nigga sticks his dick in everybody."

True enough, but the words were a direct hit to Brenda's ego and her rage was instant. In the matter of seconds, she snapped, gnashing her teeth and yelling while pointing her finger into Star's face. Game recognized game and Star knew then that there was no turning back. Brenda was trying to punk her and if she let that shit fly, the Gangstress would make her life miserable every single day until the day she graduated and left the hood behind.

Before Brenda could beat her to the punch, Star raised her fists and swung hard, hitting her with a combo two-piece. She was trying her hardest to knock Brenda's bowlegged ass right into oncoming traffic.

Wham! Wham!

"Dammn!" voices chorused around them.

Hype to see her girl throwing hands, Kevia held her hands to her mouth and jumped up and down, hooting as she watched her best friend put in work. One thing that Star did and did well was fight. Brenda wasn't on notice, but there had never been a fight that she hadn't won.

A well-calculated two-piece knocked Brenda out cold, mid-sentence, just as Star's bus pulled up. Before Brenda's friends had a chance to react, Kevia grabbed Star by her arm and pulled her onto the bus to safety.

"Think about that the next time you try to run up on me, hoe!" Star snapped, still moving. She wasn't crazy—she was moving her feet fast as hell trying to get on the bus before Brenda's crew got a chance to react.

"You knocked that hoe out!" Kevia laughed, giggling hard as the bus pulled off. "That's what I'm talkin' about. You don't let them chicks run up on you like that. You popped the shoes off that bitch!"

Stunned, Star's lips pulled into a proud smile as her best friend continued to speak, reliving the entire event as if they hadn't just gone through it only a few short moments ago. She could barely believe it herself.

With a slight turn to the window, she watched as Brenda's friends helped her up while she cried and cupped her hand under a fat and bleeding lip. Her heart filled with pride knowing that they'd all expected her to stand there and let Brenda mop up the entire block with her ass. Truthfully, there was a real possibility that Star could have gotten her ass beat but she definitely wasn't the one to stand there and wait for it.

What Star didn't know was that Brenda was part of a plan orchestrated by the Disciples, Polo specifically, to recruit her. They were supposed to scare her with the Brenda tactic and then give her the option of saving face and joining the gang instead of being jumped but it didn't get that far. They hadn't realized that Star was a hood chick at heart, with a chip on her shoulder. She'd been fighting bitches all her life, never hesitating to throw hands when she was pushed into a corner and she was good at it.

THE NEXT DAY AT SCHOOL, Star once again saw Brenda with her clique of hoes but there was also someone else there who surprised her. Tonya, Polo's chick, was with them looking like new money, dressed in all designer gear down to her shoes, blue and gold. The Gangstress were all lined up in front of the lockers, mean-mugging Star as she passed but she didn't let it get to her. Never one to show fear, she mean-mugged their asses right back and kept it moving.

"Don't pay no attention to them bitches," Kevia said as they both walked by with their heads held high. Although they didn't show a shred of fear, deep down, both of them were wondering what was really up. Tonya looked young, but she was damn near twenty-four years old. For her to be at the school about something pertaining to Star— it had to be a big deal.

"I gotta get to class," Kevia said once they got a little further down the hall. "If I'm late one more time, I'll get detention."

"Go 'head," Star told her, checking her watch. "I gotta go to the bathroom first anyways."

"Alright. After fourth period, meet me in the parking lot so we can sneak out and go to the mall. I wanna spend some of this money Sloan gave me." She smirked, and Star rolled her eyes at Kevia's spoiled ass.

Sloan was Kevia's boyfriend and was always breaking her off with some cash. Most times, she spent it on her younger brother and sisters, but every now and then, a little was left over for them to ball out. Like most caked up young niggas in their hood, Sloan was also a Disciple, but he wasn't like the rest. He was low-key, stayed to himself, and stayed out of nonsense. Every girl she and Star hung with considered their relationship as 'relationship goals' because Sloan always spoiled her. He was a gentle thug, a beast with a sensitive side that he wasn't afraid to show to his woman. It was a trait that made him easy to fall for.

"Fine. I don't wanna sit through math with Ms. Johnson's boring, salamander-looking ass anyways. We only got one exam left before graduation, so I don't know why we gotta be up in there anyways. I'll make up a reason to leave."

Playing it coy, Star snuck a glance over her shoulder and saw Brenda, Tonya, and some other foot-dragging hoes down the hall coming up behind her once Kevia walked away. She took off down the hall and waited a few paces before checking over her shoulder again.

They were gone. Good.

Falling off into the restroom before first period started, she got on Instagram as she used the bathroom, eager to check her notifications. She had recently posted a picture with her hair and makeup flawless after watching a few tutorials. Lately, she'd been getting a lot of inboxes with people asking her if they could pay her to do theirs. Her side hustle was starting to pull in major dough, she just needed more exposure.

While sitting on the toilet, looking at her phone, Star nearly fell into the bowl when she saw that a picture she'd posted had garnered over seventeen thousand likes! It was cute; she was wearing simple white booty shorts and a matching halter-top with her hair and makeup on point, but it had gone viral. 'Sexy thick' was what they were calling her in the comments. In seconds, her head swelled up big as hell.

"Oh my God!"

She bugged out when she saw that rapper, Vic Mensa, had commented on her picture. She had been stalking his page something serious, along with Polo's, day and night.

The metal bathroom door opened making a slow, screeching sound that pained her ears, but she was too caught up to pay attention to it or the murmur of voices and the clamor of approaching feet that followed.

Then somebody whispered, "Where that bitch at?" and she froze. The voice sounded familiar, making her ears perk up. Her instincts told her to look under the stall door but instead she turned back down to her phone to see what Vic Mensa had said.

He wants me to be in his next video! She could barely believe her luck.

"Whoaaaa!"

Doing her little happy dance while still sitting, she slapped her hand to her chest and read the comment about three more times. Then she just happened to look down and saw a pair of blue Balenciaga sneakers directly in front of her stall. Next to them was another pair of sneakers and another, both of them all blue and, like the other, both of them facing her stall door.

What the...?

Something told Star to get her ass up and pull her panties from around her ankles right then and this time she listened.

But it was too late.

The thin metal door of her stall flew open with a bang and it seemed like at least a thousand angry hoes jumped in on her like a herd of hungry hyenas.

"Fuck you, bitch!" one of them shouted and Star just started swinging as hard as she could, letting the punches fall where they may.

One thing for certain, it was hard as hell to fight back with her underwear wrapped around her ankles, but she managed to scuffle like a champ for a minute. That was until Tonya pulled her up out the stall by her hair and began pummeling her in the face along with the rest of her crew.

"It's the muthafuckin' Black Gangstress, bitch! Bow down!"

Their voices melded together as they shouted, almost like a chant with Tonya, the ringleader, loudest of them all.

Star's skin burned like it was inflamed and her eyes lost focus as she floated in and out of consciousness. Even months later, she would still have a hard time remembering all the details of the vicious beat down. Still, she threw her fists up to protect her face as much as she could and fought back.

As she struggled to defend herself while slowly accepting that her life might be coming to an end, all she could think was that of *all* the people she could have asked to do her dirty work, Tonya, Polo's chick and head of the Black Gangstress gang, had taken time out of her schedule to personally whip her ass. To whom did she owe the honor? Was this still about Kush, a man Star barely knew? Was this about jealousy? That couldn't *possibly* be... There was nothing about Star that Tonya had to be jealous for.

The Gangstress women rat-packed her, about ten on one, beating her like a helpless animal. Blood marred the floors and the walls but there was nothing that she could do. It was a brutal assault. They kicked and beat her as she tried to fight back and also protect her phone. To some it might sound silly—you'd have to be a teenage girl who never had shit to understand the importance of having your first iPhone.

Frantic, Star tried to resist without hitting the floor, knowing the second her back hit the ground, them grimy bitches would stump the shit out of her ass and she'd really be a wrap.

Just when she thought things couldn't get any worse, she saw something that made her heart go cold. In what felt like slow motion, an object shimmered in the white lights amidst the punch-drunk stars dancing in front of her eyes.

Hissing like a snake, Brenda pulled out a box-cutter, her face scowling and balled up beyond recognition with her deadly intent shining in her eyes. She gnashed her teeth and jerked Star's arm, trying to slice her face with the cutter. Crying out, Star blocked it with her hand and heard her phone fall to the floor as she screamed out in agony. The box-cutter sliced through her skin, making her fingers split and her ears fill with the echo of her own voice. Blood squirted like a faucet across the gray and white linoleum floor, spraying several of her attackers.

Scared into a mania, Star cried to God for mercy, but they didn't let up. She was being kicked, punched, and for some reason, Tonya still wouldn't let go of her hair as the assault continued. Yanking and pulling relentlessly, she continued to howl, "It's the fuckin' Black Gangstress, hoe!"

Star wore her nappy hair like a crown, flashing her tresses around the hood, making all the bald-headed hoes that popped shit about her weight envious of her glorious mane. It was obvious that Tonya was one of the jealous ones because she was trying her hardest to make Star just as bald-headed as she was.

"Look at your fat ass now, bitch! You ain't cute no more," somebody ranted while more feet stumped Star's body. There was *no* way this could only be about Brenda's whoring ass nigga. This was going too far. They were doing way too much.

"Pull that bitch's head up so I can cut her throat," Brenda yelled in a murky fog.

Star could see her bouncing around on the balls of her feet, hyped up, excited. Her blue coat was stained red. Somebody grabbed Star around her neck and she got frantic. They were really trying to pull her head back to slice her throat.

Just that fast things were going from childish mayhem to grown folk's murder. She was only seventeen-years-old and about to be killed in a high school bathroom only a few months short of her graduation day. What would become of her dreams then? All of her wasted potential would go down the drain in the same way as many others before her.

She'd be another statistic... a story on the evening news that people would suck their teeth and shake their heads at once they learned of how she met her fate but would soon forget as soon as the next news cycle began. So many niggas were getting bodied in the Chicago hoods that the names didn't even make the obituary section of the newspaper. To get there, you had to have been somebody much more important than a little black girl who had grown up and died on the Southside. To them, she had no future worth lamenting for.

Somehow, Star managed to thrash about as Brenda came down with the box-cutter again. She saved her neck, but the blade sliced her chest, nearly stabbing through her heart and Star suffered a nasty cut as they continued to beat her ass unmercifully.

Why do they hate me?

She was about to pass out, lying on the floor as the world strobe around her, battered with so many punches that she was certain that she would die. Death would come soon, and she would welcome it with open arms in order to escape the pain. She was losing consciousness and all her fight was gone.

"Cut that bitch in her face, too. Let that bitch know who she fuckin' with."

It was Tonya urging Brenda on.

Opening her eyes, Star saw the box-cutter inches away from her nose and then she lifted her eyes and took in an eyeful of the crazed, maniacal expression on Brenda's face.

The bitch was definitely crazy, and she meant business.

Star closed her eyes and braced herself for excruciating pain at the same exact moment that she heard the screech of metal scraping across the floor as the bathroom door opened.

Amazing grace.

In walked her fifth period math teacher, Ms. Johnson, and she had never in life been so happy to see the one teacher that she always said she couldn't stand. In a near delusional state, her lips spread into a tiny smile as she thought about the one time Kevia had deliberately passed gas while asking Ms. Johnson a question at her desk. She and Kevia had to cover their faces with their textbooks to stifle their giggles as they watched her curl up her nose at the sudden stench. Star promised God that if He spared her life, she would never terrorize Ms. Johnson again.

Walking in, Ms. Johnson held back a scream with her hands plastered over her face as she rushed over to help Star up, causing all the Gangstress to scatter and flee out the bathroom. With her teeth streaked red with blood, she watched them all scurry out the door, leaving only murky, bloody red footprints in their wake.

. . .

Ms. Johnson was able to remember most of the faces in the bathroom, which was good for her, but Star knew better and wasn't saying shit. She was rushed to the emergency room in an ambulance to St. Bernard Hospital on 64th Street where she received a total of fifty-seven stitches for her chest and hand. They also tended to her other injuries: two bruised ribs, a broken nose, and a dislocated finger but the one thing that hurt the most was knowing she'd have to wait until all that healed before she could get some payback.

With Ms. Johnson's cooperation, the police got involved but Star instantly got amnesia. In her hood snitches didn't get stitches... They got a one-way ticket to the morgue instead.

Brenda Smith and her homegirl Sheena Jackson, who had been holding Star's head back to expose her neck, were both caught, and the authorities were ready to press charges. But Star threw a serious monkey wrench into their plans when she told them that the two were not the girls that had jumped her, and she refused to press charges.

"I might need to check with Kush about getting some Percs or some shit," Star whined as she hobbled her way down the sidewalk. "My damn chest feels like it's on fire."

Cutting her eyes, Kevia gave her a sideways look. "You need to chill on messin' with dude before Brenda tries to get in your ass again. I got a cousin who can get you anything you need."

"Don't worry about it. I'm good." Star gave her a curt response, dismissing the idea as soon as it came to mind. Weed was one thing, but she vowed to never try anything stronger and end up with the same habits that plagued Roxy every single day.

It was two weeks later from the incident with the Gangstress and Star could still barely walk. Kevia had to help her get around in between classes and carry her bags. Undoubtedly, she would have been better off had she been able to see a real doctor but with no money, she was at the mercy of Roxy, whose version of insurance was slapping a Band-Aid where it hurt and saying a quick prayer to Jesus for healing.

To anyone watching, it looked like Star had been tossed out a third-floor window and she felt like it too. But it didn't stop her from going anywhere she wanted. Headstrong and as stubborn as a bull, she refused to hide even when she saw the Black Gangstress chicks lurking around. She felt the need to let them hoes know she wasn't scared. To her, courage was just a testament of growing up in the hood. At the time, she honestly didn't know that her lineage originated from an original gangsta and his blood was the same that was pumping through her veins.

THE SKY WAS a murky gray with the overcast of an impending storm. The ominous gloom cast a shadow that covered the entire city. To some, it seemed symbolic of terror to come but to those suffering through the sweltering Chicago heat, the brief reprieve from the sun was something to look forward to.

Once again, Star was at the bus stop, the same one where she had beat Brenda's ass. As usual, Kevia was right by her side but, this time, she had a big ass butcher knife hidden in her pants. The two were ready for whatever and vowed to never get caught slipping again, or so they thought, when a clique of Gangstress drove up in a tricked-out Chevy, sitting on 22s.

Behind them, two other carloads of chicks pulled up. In the last one, Star could have sworn she saw a glimpse of Polo but couldn't be certain because the windows were tinted. One thing was for certain: his crazy bitch, Tonya, was in the car with them, which she made sure to let Star know when she rolled her window down and scowled in her direction.

It would be a lie to say that Star wasn't more afraid than she'd ever been, but she held her ground. She knew she'd have to fight it out with them again, but she had been hoping that day would come when she was physically prepared, not while she was still hobbling around like a small child and just as defenseless as one. What could she possibly do to save herself now?

"Oh shit! There go them bitches Brenda and Tonya who jumped you," she heard Kevia mutter by her side, stating the obvious because there was no way *not* to see them.

Star stood stoic and watched them all hop out the car. Tonya was wearing some type of blue transparent sequin bodysuit, prominently showing her tiny pierced nipples as if she were nude. Her arms were tatted up with full sleeves. This time, she wore her long hair in a blue Mohawk, shaved down low on the sides. The top stylishly cascaded down her back as she walked ahead of the other girls, with a purpose.

"Fuck!" Star cursed, looking around for an escape plan. She thought about running but knew she was in no condition.

Walking boldly forward to protect her crippled friend, Kevia stood in the street with her hand on the butcher knife in her pants, making sure everyone knew she was strapped with something.

"Y'all bitches betta not come over here with no fuck shit. I ain't playin'!"

That was Kevia: fearless and indomitable. She lived in the Mercy Housing Projects; a thoroughbred project chick, the oldest of five with no father in the house and a mother who lived to work so that she could provide. For this reason, the responsibility of raising her siblings fell on her so protecting her loved ones was a trait that came naturally. She was like a mother hen to them and now to Star who was in no condition to help herself.

Star blew out a protracted breath and tried to calm her nerves. Even if she could put up a fight, the last ass whipping she'd endured was more than enough. Not only had the memory of that assault been beaten into her mind, she had fresh stitches in her hand, across her chest, and her ribs ached. This was no time to be brave.

Uh uh, I'll pass on this shit, she thought, looking around for some-where to run. Hopefully, Kevia's crazy ass would just follow instead of trying to be brave.

Star didn't have a death wish and not just that; her Instagram page had been blowing up even more over the last couple weeks just from putting up old pictures she already had saved in her phone. There was too much to live for. She had seen this movie before and was not in condition for a rerun.

The Gangstress all walked with so much swag, full of confidence like a silenced tidal wave about to erupt. Instantly, Star zeroed in on Tonya, squinting as sunlight peeled out through the passing clouds. Her long tresses of blue risqué hair flowed down her back, blowing in the wind. It looked like she had that good Brazilian Remy; that kind of weave cost a grip to get.

A blue and white patrol car passed by without even paying them the slightest attention. Star imagined herself running into the streets after the cop, flailing her arms in the air while asking for help. But she stood her ground because she couldn't go out like that. This was life on the Southside of the Windy City and only the strong survived. With a straight face, she simply paused and watched the cop pass by right along with everybody else.

With the threat of police intervention gone, Tonya strolled over to the girls and reached into her pocket. In the ardent sunlight, a shimmer of metal gleamed off the revolver as she pulled it out and aimed the .38 snub-nose with a pink handle right at Kevia's face and cocked it, wearing a menacing growl that could have passed for a sly grin.

That bitch is too confident now that she about three dozen hoes deep, Star thought to herself.

"What the fuck you just said, you Black ass bitch? And whatever you got in them pants better be something you can eat! Now take that shit out and throw it on the ground," Tonya spat as she glared at Kevia.

Stricken by the gun in her face, Kevia hesitated for a second.

It was as if the realization of their situation had finally dawned on her. Then she glanced over at Star. There was no fear in her face, but she didn't look absolutely fearless either.

"Bitch, I said take that shit out your pants and drop it on the ground or I'ma push your wig back with this tres-eight."

For a fleeting second, it seemed like Kevia was thinking about bucking as she scrolled her eyes once again to Star with the pistol still aimed at her face. Not speaking, she rolled her shoulders as if contemplating something.

"Kee! Thro-throw that shit on the ground!" Star whispered with a slight tremble.

She was scared that Kevia would fuck around and get killed. Gunplay was so common in the Chi that every day they expected it. Even now, Star was scared but she wasn't surprised. To her, there was nothing at all shocking about standing at the bus stop, minding your business, and then catching a bullet. Shit like that happened all the time.

With a deep sigh, Kevia tossed the butcher knife and it landed on the concrete with a clang, caroming next to one of their cars. Star followed it and caught another glimpse of a guy sitting inside the vehicle. She was almost positive that it was Polo that time and her heart jumped with a bit of hope.

What is he doing here?

In the past, Polo had always been nice to her—whenever he noticed her, that is. Once, he'd even told her that she was cute for a big girl. Beaming from ear-to-ear, Star was too young and in love to see it as anything but a compliment.

"That's what the fuck I thought, bitch!" Tonya continued, talking major shit. "Don't make me splatter yo' ass right here on this sidewalk. Y'all gone learn to recognize and respect the fact that Black Gangstress run this shit, this neighborhood, this street, this city! These streets are our fuckin' hood."

Tonya spat her venom as she bounced on the balls of her feet, all animated and antsy, putting on a show. Maybe she was high off something.

Star noticed two iced-out gold canine teeth in the bottom of her mouth sparkling in the sunlight. Then skinny ass Brenda walked up along with about six other chicks and her attention refocused onto her. She was hype as hell too.

"Yeah, y'all bitches ain't really 'bout dat life. You need to stop fakin'," she said in a singsong voice with a hint of humor in it. Then, with her lips twisted and her finger pointed at Star, she added, "But you did do somethin' kinda gangsta, bitch."

"What?" Star asked befuddled. Her voice was too high, almost strained from fear.

Brenda's crew chuckled as she continued to stare into Star as if she were looking right through her. There was a sparkle in her eyes, a glimmer of mischief, as she walked even closer. Star picked up on the scent of Febreze, Loud, and oily fish emanating from her body.

Placing her hand on her bony hip, she further explained. "You ain't snitch on us. You fought all us back and you came to school days later ready to fight again."

Brenda's lips were chapped and dry as she stared at Star with a stone-face. Star couldn't help looking at them and licked her own as she processed her words. She didn't answer but she didn't need to. Tonya gestured with the gun still aimed at Kevia and what she said next completely caught both girls off guard.

"So since you kept dat shit gangsta, we gon' give you an alternative. Y'all bitches can get jumped in and join us bangin' and become Black Gangstress or you can get jumped right here on this block, Chicago Gangland Style."

Tonya puffed up her chest and looked at her squad as she spoke her big talk. "Ain't no secret, you know how da fuck we rock—Say 'no' and get carried to the fuckin' morgue, sharing an ambulance, courtesy of the Black Gangstress. Or say 'yes' and be 'bout that life for real, runnin' shit like a G-bitch. Get money, sell dope, murk niggas, and eat good as fuck... you'll never have to worry about shit."

She threw up a gang sign and was rewarded in a ruckus response of hoots and hollers. The chicks started getting rowdy all in the streets and Star felt trapped. She felt someone push her back, then there was a harder shove. Tonya walked up to Kevia like she was about to smack her with the butt of the gun and Star's mind went into a frenzy.

Jumped in or jumped out? her mind pondered like a puzzle she couldn't solve. Kevia must have read her thoughts.

"They want us to join. Get jumped in their gang or refuse the offer and get jumped out—killed."

Eyes wide, Star gasped. Getting jumped in meant that you had to get your ass whooped as part of the initiation; a *real* beat down. Kevia had told her about some initiations she'd witness for the Black Gangstas where niggas got their teeth and eyeballs knocked out.

Using the last shred of courage she had left, Kevia decided to test their gangsta.

"Listen, I'ma have to pass on dat shit. One of my cousins is a Blood and I can't go out like that," was all she said, shaking her head.

Without hesitation, Tonya calmly strolled forward and aimed the gun at Kevia's leg, firing.

Pow!

"Oh shit! Oh shit!" Star clamored. She tried to take a timid step back, but someone pushed her from behind. A few feet from where she stood, Kevia fell to the ground crying hysterically in pain. Star wanted to help her, but she was paralyzed by her fear.

Just then, a car door slammed shut and Star looked up to see Polo getting out.

I knew it was him! she thought, her heart jumping a bit in spite of her dreadful situation. The juvenile crush that she had for this man she barely knew gave her false hope. She just knew he would be the one to save her.

Polo rushed toward them as people on the street began to run and scatter. Murderous violence had erupted in the hood right in broad ass daylight.

"Man, what the fuck you doin'!" Polo yelled, the diamond and gold grill in his mouth sparkling. There was an angry vein protruding from his forehead and Star couldn't help staring at it as it pulsed at about the same rate as her racing heart. Several of the Gangstress took a daunting step back from the wrath of their leader and just that fast, it was quiet.

"I shot that bitch! She said her cousin was a Blood, plus she didn't want to jump in—"

Before she could finish the sentence, Polo snatched Tonya around the neck with one hand, gripping her hard enough to make her expel a harsh breath.

"You was supposed to take them bitches out back in the ally, not shoot them up front and make the spot hot!"

Star flinched at being called out her name by the one man she'd spent most of her upper teenage years crushing on. But then she thought about it and figured it didn't mean anything. On their block, the word bitch was used interchangeably with 'woman', 'girl', or whatever else you were referring to.

Kevia yelled out in pain and her cries were so agonizing that Star almost felt it in her bones. She moved toward her to try to assist her friend although she had no idea what she could do, but before she could get to Kevia, a door opened from the same car that Polo had been riding in and out popped someone Star fortunately never had the displeasure of running into: Kato, the Gangster Disciple's Chief Enforcer.

Kato was tatted up with teardrops on his face and a big ass crucifix in the middle of his forehead. His hair was shaved on the sides, he wore it braided up on the top and dyed red. He stood at about six-foot-six and had a muscular, athletic physique. He looked almost identical to the rapper The Game, except much more menacing. For some reason, a lot of chicks found him attractive. Star had to admit that he was... in that 'ruthless thug' type of way. His eyes were a strange looking grayish hazel, which was kinda fly but he was always instigating trouble, and with his high-ranking position in the organization, it was like giving a madman power that he was certain to abuse.

Although she had never personally come into contact him, Star had heard many stories about Kato and none of them were good. He was a menace in the hood; the type of nigga who seemed to get off by inflicting pain on others. Innocent people were catching bullets every hour on the hour, but Kato continued to walk the streets without a care in the world as if he didn't have to answer to his own karma one day. He stalked the hood like his skin repelled bullets, but then again, with him being the main one shooting them, it made sense that he wasn't worried about catching one.

"Lay off, Polo. Ain't nothin' wrong with a little gunplay," Kato said, his eyes narrowed as he looked Star up and down, taking in her voluptuous figure.

Besides being a killer, Kato was also known for being a hoe. And his dick didn't seem to discriminate either, which made him such a hit with the ladies. If you had a pussy and a pretty face, you could get it. He was the primary example for the phrase 'community dick'. He would jump out one chick's bed and land right in her mama's if she was cute enough.

"That's just the type of bullshit I would expect you to say." Polo chuckled, looking at his best friend and right-hand man. "Yo' reckless ass wouldn't have it any other way."

Kato shrugged. "I make no apologies for bein' me."

With the attention off of her, Star took a few precarious steps toward Kevia and bent down to help her. She was holding on tight to her gunshot womb and whimpering while lying in her own blood. Tears came to Star's eyes as she watched her, feeling helpless.

"You sure she got what it take to be a Gangstress?" Kato asked with his upper lip curled in disgust. "Sittin' here 'bout to cry and shit over a simple flesh womb. Since when we started recruiting these weak ass bitches?"

Tonya tossed her head back, letting out a loud hooting laugh at Star's expense and a few of her cronies followed behind her. They were mindless followers, doing whatever they thought would get them in her good graces. Lifting her head, Star glared into Kato, hating him immediately.

"How about I shoot you in your leg so you can tell me how 'simple' it is?" she sassed before she really realized what she was saying.

Kato was on her before she could take in her next breath. With the agility of a panther, he pulled his pistol from wherever it was stashed and pointed it right at Star's calf muscle, his finger on the trigger.

"You first," he said, his voice so cold that Star's entire body froze. The look in his eyes dared her to call his bluff. They stared into each other's eyes for what felt like an infinite moment in time, neither one willing to back down.

His irises were lit with a wicked flame that was taunting in nature; almost as if he were wishing she would make a wrong move so that he could pull the trigger. Star felt her heart go still in her chest but she refused to cower under his glare. He was searching for fear and she was set on not giving him the pleasure of seeing an ounce of it in her. His type lived off inflicting terror.

She jutted her chin out, appearing much bolder than she felt and the edge of Kato's lips curled up in a cruel smirk. She was a soldier, true enough, but he felt like trying her. Running his tongue along his bottom row of teeth, he prepared to push down on the trigger.

Just then, as if on cue, they heard it.

Police sirens wailed around them as Kevia lay in fetal position on the ground in a newly formed puddle of her own blood. A shred of sunlight broke through the dark sky at the same time that a cop car bent the corner, driving toward them. It was Star's saving grace. Niggas took off like roaches with the lights on, leaving only her and a howling Kevia behind.

Kato was the last to retreat, tucking his gun in the small of his back while he continued to glare down at her. He was somewhat impressed by the young girl who showed more courage than any man who had been on the wrong side of his gun but part of him knew she wasn't as brave as she appeared.

"We'll meet again," he said to her with a menacing half-smirk. His icy words were every bit of a threatening promise that he'd soon fulfill.

Chuckling a little to himself, he gave her one last long look before turning to jump back into the whip with Polo. It was then that Star was able to finally let out the breath she'd been holding.

STAR AND KEVIA were officially made Black Gangstress that same day. It wasn't a matter of choice but a requirement of living in the concrete jungle known as the Chi.

Since Star had already gotten her ass whooped at school and Kevia had been shot in the leg, their initiation requirement was to shoot and rob a rival gang member by the name of Creflo. Star had never in her life shot anybody or thought that she would, but it came down to choosing either his life or hers and she did what she had to do in order to save her own ass.

She wasn't the bravest Gangstress to ever do it, but she did whatever needed to be done. And no one could question that.

CHAPTER 3

Back to the Present

STAR'S MIND WAS REELING AS SHE RUSHED OVER AND TOOK HER grandmother by the elbow, leading her down the hall. The sound of her walker scraping across the old wooden floor was nerve-wracking as she looked over her shoulder and saw Roxy pushing and shoving Steve toward the front door for him to answer it. It did nothing to slow her pace, the only thing Star cared about right then was saving her granny and little sister.

Bam! Bam! Bam!

It sounded like somebody was knocking on the door with the butt of a gun.

"Yo! Star, answer the door," a voice called out from the other side; it sounded like Mink. Pressing on, Star's legs moved faster directing her grandmother to safety. She wouldn't be able to get her out the back door, so she had no choice but to hide her in her own room.

"Child, what's going on and why you in such a hurry?" Geraldine asked, causing her oxygen mask to fog up. She had her own suspicions about what kind of trouble her granddaughter was mixed up in but wanted to hear it from Star herself.

"Granny, my mama did something bad. Some guys are about to come in here, and they might be mad at her. I want you to stay in your room with the door shut—"

"Uh uh, hell naw! I'm not staying in my room. This is *my* house. I pay the rent up in here, so how about *y'all* asses leave! Ever since y'all come to live with me, it's been hell, and yo' mama don't pay no rent anyway."

"Granny, I can handle it. Just go in your room and shut the door, please," Star persuaded, nudging her toward her bedroom door. The knocking on the front door got so loud it made the walls rumble.

"I'm comin'!" Star shouted to the top of her lungs. That's when she noticed Geraldine's eyes bulge wide. She had finally seen the small .380 pistol in Star's hand.

"Oh Lawd, Jesus, help me," she said pensively, and her body seemed to go slack as she leaned fully on her walker. Her frail body began to shiver as she spoke.

"This is too much! You gon' end up sending me to my grave early. First, your mama, and now you. What's goin' on, child?" she said with a frown and placed her little hand on Star's shoulder. It felt like God Himself had touched her because suddenly she was filled with emotions that made it hard to speak.

"Granny, I'ma be okay, just wait in here... I'ma come back and get you, I promise," Star said with a plea in her voice.

She couldn't even look her grandmother in her face, because she knew in her heart that there was a strong chance that she would never see her again. Then something dreadful dawned on her. Among all the rambling Roxy had been doing in her room, she'd admitted that she had stashed the drugs under her grandmother's mattress. Star thought about moving it or simply giving it back to Mink, but her mind was all over the place.

Bam! Bam! Bam!

Gently shutting the door behind her, Star swallowed the dry lump in her throat and walked down the hall to peek in on her sister. She was in her room, still asleep. Thank God. Maybe she could just settle all of this, and they would all be spared.

Running up the hall to the sound of more pounding on the door,

Star's mind was racing. There was a serious struggle going on between Roxy and Steve. Roxy had a large butcher knife in her hand, threatening him.

"Do what the fuck I say, or I'ma poke your ass with this blade!"

With that, she shoved him so hard it looked like a punch as he stumbled backward to the front of the apartment. To Star's horror, she watched as Steve turned around and opened the door.

Big fuckin' mistake!

CHAPTER 4

THE DOOR OPENED, AND ROXY TOOK OFF RUNNING DOWN THE HALL like a track star, leaving Steve shaking like a leaf on a tree. He actually peed down his leg; Star watched it drip onto the floor.

"Nigga, where our fucking dope and money?"

The voice belonged to Kato. The gruffness of it sent a shiver down Star's spine. Right then, she actually felt sorry for Steve, but she was also thankful that she wasn't in his shoes.

"I'on-I'on... I-I dunno what'cha talkin' 'bout!" Steve stuttered with his hands up in the air.

Pow! Pow!

Kato let off two quick shots and Steve folded up, crumpling to the floor like a tin can before falling into a fetal position. Mink began to kick and punch him violently as Kato and Shawn, another lieutenant, barged their way in. Star's heart beat so fast in her chest that it felt like she was going to vomit it up.

"Where the fuck is yo' mama at?" Kato asked. His face was a ball of anger, with his eyebrows knotted up in a tight line across his forehead. In his hand was a smoking .9 mm and he was ready to use it once more. Behind him was now Mink, Polo's baby brother, and crazy ass Shawn.

Shit! He's a hitta, Star thought, looking at the AK-47 at Shawn's side.

"I dunno where my mama at. I was sleepin' until y'all niggas started beatin' on the door," Star lied with a straight face. "Why?"

"That bitch and that nigga by the door stole our dope and money," he said as a matter of fact.

Dismissing her for the moment, Kato pushed by, followed by Mink and Shawn. The AK-47 at Shawn's side had black tape around it. Star learned later that the black tape was part of a makeshift silencer. She looked back toward the front door. Steve was sprawled on the floor, seemingly dead.

Oh shit! her mind screamed.

"Where you goin? W-What y'all doin'?" Her voice was resonating with panic.

"We looking for your mama and our shit," Kato replied nonchalantly as he continued walking, looking in rooms. His hands were bloody as he breathed heavily. Star stole another glance behind her at Steve who was lying motionless.

Is he dead? she thought to herself.

Her mind instantly fell on Kato. He was the one guy who had wanted her initiation to be that she was gangbanged by all Disciples. It was Polo who had talked him out of it. Kato was the perfect choice for a Chief Enforcer, and he carried out the role well. He had an 'I don't give a fuck attitude', was crazy as the devil, and just as brutal as the principle law of the land: kill or be killed. Together, Kato and Shawn were responsible for about a dozen homicides and hundreds of gunshot victims. But Kato was the worst of them all; he was a natural born killer.

"Bitch, if we find your mama, that dope, or that money in this house, you getting violated. I'ma put a hot one through your fuckin' dome on the spot."

Kato's fetid breath smelled of alcohol and Loud as he tried to steal a look down her torn housecoat. The threat of a violation made Star's blood run cold. A violation was the worst punishment you could get in a gang and almost always ended in death after pure torture.

"I—I don't know what you're talkin' 'bout. She ain't here."

Star cut her eyes to Mink, giving him a silent plea for help. As

Polo's brother, he had shown her some kindness a few times in the past. It was her hope that she'd be able to appeal to that. Careful not to make any sudden movements, she eased her trembling hand into her nightgown to grab the pistol.

The men all marched by, searching the house. They were headed toward her sister Ebony's room when Star could no longer hold in her screams. She had to stop them from going any further.

"That's my sister's room! What y'all doin'?"

"Fuck you mean! We lookin' for your crack-head ass mama and our fuckin' dope," Kato said as she watched him walk into her baby sister's room. Star rushed down the hall after them, praying that Roxy was not in there hiding.

As soon as she entered the room, she saw that Kato had the light on and had snatched the covers off of Ebony's body. She was partially nude with only her panties and bra on.

"Damn, she ain't got shit on," Kato said, looking her up and down with a lustful eye. He licked his lips and paused, helping himself to a good look.

"Chill, nigga, that's a baby. She's a little girl," Mink admonished, then glanced at Star with apologetic eyes.

"I doubt that. Ain't nothin' little on her," Kato replied, reaching out like he was about to grab Ebony. She shrunk away from his hand, and Star nearly lost it.

"She ain't but thirteen years old. Leave her alone!"

It was a lie. Ebony was actually fifteen but telling Kato that may have sealed her fate. There were fourteen-year-olds walking around the hood with big ass pregnant bellies. Once a girl made it to fifteen, she was damn near grown. She had never heard of Kato messing with a girl so young but Star couldn't be sure of what he was capable of.

Petrified, Ebony took one look at Star and dashed away from the bed, rushing over and hugging her for dear life.

"Star, what they doing in here?" she asked with her eyes ablaze with fear.

"Lil' bitch, tell us where your mother at!" Kato raged, looking under the bed. He got agitated and just pulled the entire mattress up, tossing it on the floor before turning on Ebony, staring at her expectantly.

"We don't know where she at! Why y'all tearing up my stuff? Get out of my room!" Ebony sassed boldly like Star had taught her to do when in danger. But this wasn't the time to be talking big shit.

"You better tell this miniature hoe to shut up before I slap the shit outta her ass!" Kato shouted to Star who grabbed Ebony even tighter in her arms.

Spewing a string of curse words from his lips, Kato began to destroy the room even more, turning over furniture and chairs, looking for the money and drugs. He knocked over lamps, kicked at her stuffed animals, leaving nothing but destruction in his wake.

"Why don't you all stop it? My mama ain't here!"

"You fuckin' lying!" Kato snapped and reached back, slapping Star so hard that her neck snapped back. Instantly, her hand went for the gun, but Ebony was standing too close between them, staring at her older sister with doe eyes, etched in the terror of the moment.

"You fuckin' hit me, nigga!" Star gnashed her teeth as she spoke and balled up her fists. Kato peeped the move and was on her before she could even think of retaliating back.

"Bitch, I'll punch your ass like a fuckin' man and then pop a hot one right between your eyes. Keep on talkin'," Kato stated while Shawn grinned slyly like he was getting some enjoyment out of her suffering.

"Nigga, chill. We lookin' for our product and her mama, that's it. Until then, no drama," Mink admonished, his diamond grill sparkling as he spoke.

Star looked at him with gracious eyes, thankful that he intervened. Next to him, Kato was far less enthused, but he backed down because Mink was superior to him in rank. Still, he felt the need to grunt out a final threat.

"Star, if I find out you had something to do with this, you will be violated, and it's going to be the *worst* ever. I put that on God. So you might as well just tell me where your mama and that product is right now. You talk, and we'll take it easy on you," Kato said. He was staring at her breasts as if he were talking only to them.

Star could hardly speak; her words came out twisted in bunches, like she was regurgitating.

"How y'all know my mama stole something from y'all?" she asked in a high-pitched tone that even sounded strange to her own ears, as Ebony held on tight to her waist, trembling. She had a blanket wrapped around her shoulders, but her shivers were from fear.

"Because your mama was the last person to cop some dope from us, and somebody saw her and Steve walking around in back of the house," Kato replied. "And if y'all don't start talkin' soon, everyone in this bitch finna be laid out just like that muthafucka."

"But my grandma, my baby sister, and I ain't did nothing wrong! Plus, I'm on count now—I'm officially a Gangstress. Y'all can't just walk up in here and threaten us without good reason," Star pleaded poignantly, focusing all her attention on Mink who was the most rational of the three.

"We can do what the fuck we want! This order came down from Polo, the governor," Kato boasted.

Horrified, Star cut her eyes at Mink for affirmation. He gave her a subtle nod with his lips pressed tight. Kato's words knocked the wind out of her, like a low punch to her gut.

Polo ordered this? she thought.

She didn't understand it. Ever since ordering her initiation, he'd kept a close eye on her, and she thought it was because he liked her. Part of being a Gangstress was that you had to cut dope for the Disciples. Polo would specifically ask for her to come down to the trap to perform the task whenever he was around. They would often exchange glances, and she'd even caught him staring at her with admiration while she worked on more than one occasion. He couldn't possibly have ordered a hit on her family.

"So you might as well tell us where the dope and money is because if we find it, it's over for you. Closed casket, feel me?" Kato threatened, looking between Ebony and Star.

Again, she glanced over at Mink, and he gave her a blank stare. This time, it became obvious he was not coming to their rescue.

For a fleeting second, she actually thought about giving them the money stashed in her closet, in hopes that they would take it easy on her and leave her family alone. Then she thought about her little sister and knew that she couldn't give in and leave her to navigate through the world alone. So she said nothing.

"Go search the rest of the house." Mink barked orders, and Star watched Kato do an about-face, turning around to march his ass right into their grandmother's room.

Her heart seemed to shrink in her chest, and then the commotion began. Star nearly fainted when she heard Geraldine scream to the top of her lungs, yelling for Kato to get out. Then she heard a loud hit, the sound of skin smashing against skin, and her blood went ice cold.

"Bitch, shut your old ass the fuck up!" Kato raved, and Star took off for the room with the quickness. So did Mink, Shawn, and Ebony.

"Chile, dis man done hit me!" Geraldine said, holding the side of her face. Her mouth was bloody; her breathing apparatus was hanging from her face sideways, and her silver hair was bunched all to one side.

That was it. Star completely lost it, and every ounce of her fear turned into rage. It was like she was having a horrific out of body experience. Before she knew it, her hand reached inside her pocket, and she came out with the gun, aimed it, and shot Kato in the face at point blank range. The bullet tore through his forehead, knocking out a patch of red hair. Blood and matter sprayed her gown as he fell, head first, onto the floor.

Just as she turned, nearly too late, Mink was standing to her right with his brow knotted across his face. He reached for his strap and was about to pull out and shoot, but she was faster. Things seemed to move in slow, surreal motion. She shot him once, then twice. The first bullet hit him in the chest, making him slightly take several steps back. Still, he continued to pull at his gat, but the next bullet struck him in the cheek, causing him to stagger backward on his back, right next to Geraldine's breathing machine. He landed against the wall and slid down, a trail of blood spilling from multiple holes in his body.

"Crazy bitch!" Shawn yelled. His eyes were blood red as he aimed the AK-47 at Star and prepared to shoot.

She pivoted, but she saw the gun too late. Her whole life flashed before her eyes. She would never forget what it was like looking down the barrow of an assault rifle... staring death right in the face.

CHAPTER 5

IT WAS AS IF A GIANT HAND HAD KNOCKED THE WIND OUT OF Shawn, causing him to stagger forward and expel a deep, exacerbated breath as his eyes fulgurated terror. Then came a strained, winded, guttural sound that escaped his lungs; he gagged with his eyes spread wider as crimson blood trickled from his mouth and his lips moved without words. The assault weapon fell to the floor, and soon he followed it, lying face down on top of it. That's when Star saw the big ass butcher knife poking out of his back. Behind him stood Roxy, with a maniacal expression on her face. This was something straight out a horror movie, but worse.

"Oh-gud-Jesus-help-mi-lawd!" Geraldine crooned as she gripped her chest, fingers entwined. Her mouth was bloody, her face pale as a sheet. In the background standing behind Roxy was Ebony. She stood frozen as if paralyzed by fear.

Star couldn't help but gasp when she saw the big ass butcher knife sticking out of Shawn's back. Then she looked back at Roxy and the deranged look on her face. She had possibly saved the lives of the entire family, but Star still saw one big problem. They were standing in a house that held the bodies of three slain high-ranking Disciples while a crew of others were waiting outside. What in the hell was she going to do?

"What we gon' do now?" Roxy asked in a shaky voice filled with dread and despair.

The gun was still in Star's hand as she looked around at the bodies scattered on the floor, a river of blood galore. Then she realized that Kato was still breathing. She watched his chest rise and fall. Instinctively, she knew that she needed to shoot him again but couldn't. She didn't have the heart for it but her entire family was watching... She had to do something.

A phone began to ring.

It was some type of ringtone to a rap song that Star had never heard before. They all looked around trying to figure out where the sound was coming from, and then it dawned on them all. It was Mink's phone; the ringtone was coming from his pocket. Star could actually see the phone glowing blue as it rang.

"Shit! Shit!"

"Want me to take it out his pocket and answer it?" Roxy asked while frantically looking around. Star could tell she was still high.

"NO!"

There was the sound of a car door slamming outside, and Star took off for the window to look outside. Behind her, Roxy stooped down next to Kato, taking off his thick gold diamond chain and ruffling through his pants pockets. She removed a wad of cash as Ebony looked on, innocent eyes gleaming with horror in all the chaos as tears streaked her pretty face.

As Star pulled back the curtain, a roach scurried up the wall, but she was so overcome with fright that she barely even noticed it. Her heart dipped between her lungs and then bounced back up, making her nauseated, as she peered outside. There stood Polo with his cell phone to his ear looking right up at the window. He was surrounded by at least twenty other Disciples, his soldiers. There was a lot of activity and movement out on the street. Hood niggas became restless at the possibility of impending war. It was exciting, nerve-racking. They knew somebody was about to die tonight, and it made them antsy.

Star's phone chimed in her pocket, and she quickly grabbed it and looked at the screen.

It was Polo. She nearly pissed down her leg, just like Steve.

"Oh God! Oh God," she repeated over and over while doing a two-step like she was walking in place. Her nerves were like an electrical current ravishing her entire body.

"Fuck!"

She was about to let the curtain close when she suddenly saw Polo frantically gesturing with his arms as he spat orders, pointing at her apartment building. Then he removed a gun from his pants and took off in a trot, headed right for the apartment, followed by one of his goons.

Star was petrified! In the face of danger and overcome with stress, she transformed into a small child and started wailing for the help of her mother.

"Mama, Polo and all them on they way upstairs, now!"

Hysteria was building with each moment like an avalanche about to erupt. She covered her face with her hands in anguish and nearly fell to the floor. On the other hand, Roxy had the paranoia that came with being a dope fiend and her trained ears had picked up on a sound that Star's had missed. Rushing over to the window, she nearly knocked her own daughter through it.

"Oh fuck, here they come, Star! Now we in real trouble," Roxy warned, not telling her something she didn't already know.

"I know. Polo is out there and—"

"Girl, I'm not talkin' about no damn Polo. CPD just pulled up in a caravan of cars, and they deep as fuck!"

What? The cops!

Star ran and pulled back the curtain. Their block was like a hostile third world nation, infamously named Chiraq, by the ones who didn't live there, and for a good reason. It may have been one of the only places in the world that did not discriminate. Whether you were a woman or man, child, or senior citizen, you could get it with a free ride to the morgue if you were in the wrong place at the wrong time.

The police rolled up like the SWAT team, and she quickly noticed Polo and his crew running in the opposite direction, to their trap house across the street. Star had a momentary sigh of relief that was short-lived when several white cops jumped out of their patrol cars and ran up the steps toward the apartment building, while another group ran around back. Instantly, Star knew that nothing good was going to come out of this. White cops in a Black neighborhood were like an invasion of the Klan. Legally, they would shoot first and talk shit later. 'Guilty until proven innocent' seemed to be their motto when it came to niggas, especially in the hood.

Star didn't have a clue as to what to do except to protect her baby sister. She peeled Ebony's shivering hands off her body and spoke to her sternly like she wasn't terrified out of her mind for her own life.

"Go get in your bed, and you better stay there. Don't move, and if anybody asks you shit, tell them you was sleep, you don't know shit, you didn't hear shit, or see shit. You understand?" Star raised her voice as she mopped at her tears with the back of her hand. Ebony nodded and then hugged her older sister. Muffling her cries, she took off for her room.

Just then, there was a loud knock at the door followed by the sporadic crackle of police radios, metal arsenals, and caustic voices. Shit was about to get real!

Without any other recourse, Star had no choice but to forget about herself and protect her family. It was a scary task, but she'd always felt like the one in charge of making sure her loved ones were straight, so she was prepared. Just the thought of it took some of the weight off her back. A small bit anyways.

Dejected, she hung her head and headed for the door. She would just tell the cops the truth and suffer the consequences of her actions. Roxy was really the one to blame, but even though she was a junkie, she was still Star's mama, and she loved her. She would never give her up.

As she walked by Geraldine, the old woman grabbed her grand-child's arm so tight that it made Star wince as she whirled her around.

"Where you think you goin', girl?" she asked, her oxygen mask fogged with her dismay.

"I'ma-I'ma just tell-tell the cops I did everything," Star said, stumbling over her words, with a suffocating feeling of anxiety over-whelming her as her bottom lip trembled.

The pit of her gut churned. All the while in her peripheral, she could see Roxy jerk her neck up to look at her as she took several steps closer. She still had Kato's money and jewelry in her hand.

"Ain't no way in hell the cops gon' believe you shot two dudes and stabbed the other one, and I damn sho' ain't finna tell 'em I did it. So you better come up with a better idea than that, or else my ass gon' be sitting in a cell!" Roxy snapped and looked toward the room with the bodies in it.

In the background, Ebony was sobbing.

"You ain't gon' tell the police that story, that's for damn sure," Geraldine said, then continued. "The white man don't know nothin' but how to lock your ass up. You will end up just like your daddy. He already in jail on death row. fighting for his life. Now you tryna be there too."

Star didn't have a clue what she was rambling on about, but when she finally found out, her entire world would be forever changed.

"What you gon' do is grab that poor man that them fools shot up." She pointed at Steve lying on the floor with a smoldering hole in his chest.

"Put him in the room, take your gun, and place it in his hand. Make it look like there was a shootout, and they killed each other. I'll tell them that is what I saw and that I stabbed the other boy in his back after he hit me," Geraldine said and hobbled off, maneuvering with her walker out the room, leaving them all to stare stupefied at her.

When she returned, they all looked on in horror. She was holding the bloody butcher knife; there was smeared blood on her nightgown and hands.

"It's niggas killing niggas, so they don't really care to do anything that will make their job hard. I'm an old woman that was assaulted by Black men—gang members. Who you think they gon' believe?"

They all just looked at her in awe.

"Now you just do what I say. Keep yo' mouth shut, and don't be talkin' too much, because the police like to write shit down."

As soon as she said it, the sound of the police nearly trying to tear down the door alarmed them all.

Bam! Bam! Bam!

"This is the Chicago Police! We got probable cause to knock this fucking door down. Now open up!"

"Oh God, I—" Roxy was about to say something, but Geraldine cut her off.

"If you don't get your Black ass down there and help that girl drag that boy in the room, I'ma whip yo' Black ass like Ike! What, you tryin' to wait until them crackas kick the door in?"

She jumped to do as she was told. As soon as they had placed Steve's body in the room and positioned the gun in his hand, the front door came crashing in.

"Chicago Police Department! Put your hands up where we can see them!" the cops shouted as they stormed in.

Star lifted her hands in the air and bit down on her trembling bottom lip as tears pooled in the corners of her eyes. Never had she been so scared in her entire life.

CHAPTER 6

G<small>ERALDINE WAS RIGHT</small>.

When it came to niggas killing niggas, especially when it looked gang related, the Chicago police often went with the quickest path to 'justice' without investigating further. They took the made-up story, hook line and sinker, without question or suspicion. After they'd taken the statements and removed the bodies from Geraldine's home, they left, and Star was able to relax.

Well... not too much.

She was smart enough to know that the police were the least of their worries. She still had to deal with Polo and the other GD's. Not even an hour after the coast was clear, he summoned Star and Roxy to the trap house. As they were escorted by a crew of Gangstress, her heart raced like an Olympic track star. Was this going to be the last night of her short little life?

Somewhere in the trap, a Drake song direfully played, and the lights were dim. There was a stench of musk, cheap cologne, and fear mingling with Loud smoke as Star stumbled in and nearly fell. She strained her eyes to adjust to the dim light. All the way across the room, there was a figure—a silhouette of a man—but it was eerie. He was bound and tied, lying on his side. She could vaguely make out a body.

"Come on, P. I ain't did shit, man. Untie me," a voice groaned painfully. "We grew up as homies. Why you gotta do this to me?"

"Shut the fuck up, nigga!" Polo barked.

He turned and looked between Star and Roxy with a menacing glare, his dreads hanging down his back. His face was etched in disgust like he had pure hatred for them, and his eyes were bloodshot red and swollen. He was in distress and terrifying but was still dressed to the nines in a white Gucci hoodie, True Religion jeans, and white Gucci shoes. His iced-out platinum and diamond GD chain sparkled with an array of luminous colors. If it was her time to go, Star was grateful to at least see such a gorgeous sight before the tragic deed was done.

As she took everything in, she heard the shuffle of feet, many feet, and the murmur of harsh voices almost in acoustic drones. It was then that it dawned on her there was a coliseum of niggas in the spot, all watching for what was to come next. As protocol would suggest, Polo had called for an emergency meeting. There had to be at least a hundred niggas cramped into the basement type structure. It once serviced as the utility section of the building, but it had been trans-formed into a dungeon type 'trap house' or a death den, which is what it felt like that day.

The Gangstress that had escorted Star and Roxy in, all strolled over to their section of the spot and watched attentively, everyone except Tonya. She walked to Polo and began to caress his back with an affec-tionate hand. On her lips, she wore a satisfied smirk, happy to see Star in the situation that she was in. Polo abruptly pulled away from her like he was aggravated and continued to focus on Star and Roxy, who was shivering with fright.

"I'ma make an example outta both of you right now if somebody don't tell me somethin'," he began with his upper lip curled maliciously. "What the fuck happened to my brother?"

Like a floodgate, Roxy was talking a hundred miles a minute.

"You know I wouldn't do anything to you or your brother. I love y'all like my own family. Every morning you give me a hit to get my day started, and I do everything you need me to do. I go get food for your dog, feed him, go to the store for you, watch out for the cops... I ain't never done nothin' wrong to *or* your brother. Y'all are like family!" she rambled on, both crying and talking at the same time. It would have been an epic performance had Polo believed her.

Pow!

He slapped her so hard that Star almost felt it as Roxy staggered, nearly falling.

"What the fuck happened in that house with my brother!" Polo yelled so loud his voice echoed as he pointed a gun at her head and cocked it.

Star was horrified. He was preparing to shoot her mother, execution-style, right in front of her. She was shocked, but at the same time, she really wasn't. It was well-known in the hood that Polo didn't give a fuck about anyone when it came to his money. His own mama could get it if she touched his stash.

Standing next to Roxy as she collected herself, Star remained silent and waited for her to continue to speak.

"Huh? Oh, uh-uh... they came and knocked at the door, and um... Kato shot Steve. Then they came in..."

Star stared at her in horror. Roxy must have been punch-drunk because her ass was telling Polo what had actually happened instead of the same story they'd told the police.

"If Kato shot Steve, then how in da fuck did my brother get killed?" Polo raved.

Thinking quickly, Star intervened and stood in front of Roxy like she was prepared to take a bullet, but really, she was trying to shut her ass up.

"Kato did shoot Steve and then Steve shot back. They shot each other—"

Polo glared at her, his eyes void of any affection he may have had for her only days before. His only brother was dead, and someone had to pay for that crime. No matter what he may have felt about Star before, in this moment, she was the enemy. Polo had no other family in the world besides Mink; the lifestyle he'd been born into had taken out everyone close to him a long time ago, and now, his brother was gone too, and someone had to pay.

Reaching out, Polo grabbed Star by her throat with his massive hand, cutting off the air to her windpipe. She couldn't breathe; all she could do was gurgle words inaudibly as he nearly lifted her off her feet, shoving her hard against the wall before releasing her.

With his other hand, he turned and then leveled the gun on Roxy and twisted his face into a ball of anguish. He was just about to squeeze the trigger when Star jumped and started talking fast as she could.

"The place was small, cramped. It all happened in my grandma's room. Kato slapped my grandmother, then Steve came in to help her, but Kato shot him. Steve managed to shoot back, gunfire was exchanged, and somehow, your brother got shot," she said, winded. Maybe for the first time in her life, she was a faster talker than Roxy.

"My brother was shot twice, once in the face and once in the chest. This shit ain't adding up," Polo rebutted.

"But it's the truth!" Roxy and Star said in unison.

Everyone in the spot was quiet except the guy tied up on the other side of the room. He continued to moan and plead for Polo to untie him.

Polo stared at them, his mind working over the details of their story, and it seemed like he may have been thinking of letting them go. Then Tonya, seeing the anger and rage leaving from her man, decided to jump in.

"Bae, don't trust that bitch—either of them. Ain't neither one said shit about Shawn getting stabbed in the back, so they both lying."

With her comment came a chorus of the Gangstress trying to co-sign what she was implying. Star shivered as she listened to the ruckus around her while peering into Tonya's malicious and cold eyes. She was on to them and knew they were lying. Or maybe her hatred of Star was what fueled her. She'd noticed the way Polo looked at the young girl's curvaceous body and was more than ready to rid the world of her. All competition had to be squashed, and in her mind, that was exactly what Star was.

"My grandma stabbed Shawn! I told you they was all in a small ass room, and they had assaulted her. She was only trying to protect herself. She's eighty years old!" Star yelled. Her voice was a falsetto of fear. She needed to stop the madness before it really got started.

"That bitch lying, bae. Shoot her and her mama. Just get it over with," Tonya persuaded with envy in her eyes.

"If Kato slapped her eighty-year-old grandmother, she had every right to defend herself. The bylaws of the organization states we are prohibited from hitting elderly. That is a violation," a thick baritone voice said.

It was Sloan, Kevia's boyfriend. He was second in command behind Polo. The two bumped heads a lot, and normally, he wouldn't have stepped in since this was some personal shit now that Mink was dead, but he couldn't stand by and let Star or Roxie be hurt right in front of his face. Kevia would never forgive him.

"That bitch is lying. I'm tellin' you! Kato would have *never* hit an elderly woman," Tonya said casually walking up. She had a pistol in her hand.

"Shit... like hell! Kato's crazy ass shot at his own mama once!" someone cut in.

With Tonya at his side, looking like a venomous snake, Polo stared into Star with an intensity that made it feel as if she were being sliced in two by a laser. Time seemed to lull as her fate hung in the balance.

Would he kill her? Would she die at the hands of the one man on Earth she'd spent most of her adolescent life crushing on? Time seemed to pass as slow as molasses running up a hill. She could barely take the stress of it all and vowed right then that if she ever got the chance to leave this gang shit behind her, she wouldn't hesitate to take it.

"Due to your status as a Gangstress, I'll take you on your word... for now," Polo said, and a rush of relief passed over Star's body. Then in the next instant, it was taken away as he continued.

"Kato is still alive... He's in a coma, but they say that he'll soon be awake. Once that happens, we'll know the truth."

Without even looking at her, Star felt Roxy's body tense up beside her, and she knew they were thinking the same thing. Once Kato awoke and told Polo the details of what had really happened that night, their fates would be sealed. Polo would kill them both in cold blood without blinking an eye. It didn't matter that her grandmother had been attacked or that Star was simply protecting her family. She would die a merciless death, and her entire family would probably be extinguished as well.

In a matter of days, her whole world had taken a sudden turn. At seventeen-years-old, she should've been living her best life, getting ready for her eighteenth birthday, preparing for her senior prom, and getting excited about graduation while spending her nights still dreaming about a man who barely knew she existed. But now, none of that was important anymore. The gang life had stolen her future, and she had to come up with a plan to snatch it back.

Or else, she would die.

CHAPTER 7

Two Months Later

STAR RAN HER THUMB OVER THE SCREEN OF HER BRAND-NEW PHONE, reading each new comment that she'd received on her latest photos. Being an Instagram model wasn't anything close to what she wanted for her life, but it turned out that it was something she was good at. With wide hips and a small enough waist to make her ass impossible to miss, she realized that the extra pounds she'd spent most of her life trying to cover up were now her most prized possession. In only a few months, she'd taken a hobby and flipped it into a dream... People were paying her to promote their businesses on her page, she was getting messages about appearing in videos, and her schedule was booked for the next two weeks with girls wanting her to do their hair and makeup.

With prom approaching, she had high expectations of making more money than she'd ever planned to when she did her first makeup tutorial online, and to say she was geeked about that was a terrible understatement. Every dollar that came in was either reinvested back into her business for more makeup and clothes, or it was locked away in her safe to go toward her college fund. No matter what she had going on around her, she held on to the goal of making it out of the

Southside so that she could get into somebody's college, Northwestern being her primary choice.

"Bitch, what you doin' for your birthday? We need to rent out like three hotel rooms and get lit all night long! My cousin can get us everything we need, plus, his homeboy works at a hotel, so he can get us one real cheap," Kevia said with her hands waving in the air, all animated as she spoke.

Although her eyes were on Star's face, her mind's eye was already thinking about the major turn-up that she had in mind. The best dancer on the block, Kevia, was always ready for a party. She loved any opportunity to shake her hips, smoke a little somethin', and sip on a little something else. Being the oldest of five children and the daughter of a woman who worked fourteen-hour days only to come home and drop right into the bed at night, Kevia spent most of her time raising kids that weren't hers and jumped at any opportunity to let loose.

They were sitting outside on Star's front stoop, still in their school clothes, just chilling. Star had about an hour before her next customer was supposed to come through to get her makeup done, and she couldn't wait. This would be the money she would use to buy the dress that she planned to wear. It was a long form-fitting gown that hung onto every single one of her curves, showing off the body that she was growing more accustomed to showing off after seeing all the attention that she was getting online. She didn't have a date, but that was the least of her worries. As soon as she stepped into the room, she was fully confident that all eyes would be on her and her alone. The girl who had been teased and poked fun at all her life, would finally come out on top.

"What them niggas over there doin'?" Kevia asked, pulling Star out of her daydream of how wonderful her prom night would be, and she followed her eyes across the street.

There stood Polo, standing outside of the trap house with a few of his goons, and he was looking right at her as he also watched the streets like a hawk. The day was bustling with people; mostly crackheads, hustlers, and the ordinary dope fiends. There was a rowdy dice game in progress on the side of the building. One could get the impression that something ominous loomed, but then again, this was the Chi;

even on such a spectacular day, paranoia was always palpable like a sixth sense, a safeguard against death.

Star's heart leapt a little in her chest, and she couldn't help but bite down on the corner of her bottom lip to calm the beating of her heart as she watched Polo's movements. He was just so *fine.*

The past couple months, her nerves had been on edge after everything that had gone down that one horrible night, and since then, Polo still held her in suspicion, at least he seemed to, but on rare occasion, she would catch him ogling her body and giving her a lascivious, sly grin. The jury was still out on what he thought regarding Mink, but what was very clear was he was a dude that was interested in her in a way that was obvious like a sexual gravity pull.

For the most part, he had been nice to her, so she tried her best to no longer worry that he didn't believe her take on how everything went down with his brother's murder. The threat of it all was imminent, but it was also an allure, just like his imperturbable thug-appeal. Fire was beautiful, but it could also burn you—it could kill, and so would Polo if he ever found out the truth.

"Don't tell me you still caught up by that crazy nigga," Kevia said with a snort, noting the far away, glazed over look in Star's eyes. A goofy grin crossed her face, but she made no moves to respond.

"Aye, didn't he slap Roxy?"

Star sucked her teeth and gave Kevia a sideways look. "I wanted to slap her ass, too! The whole reason we were even in that predicament in the first place was because of *her*, and then she almost messed it all up again by tellin' Polo the truth."

With raised brows, Kevia had to nod her head at that. When Star finally relaxed enough to tell her everything that had actually gone down the night of Mink's murder, she could barely believe that she was able to make it out of there alive. Plenty of people had met the end of their existence behind the barrel of Polo's pistol and for much less.

Polo was a dangerous man, but from the look in Star's eyes as she ogled him in broad daylight, she didn't seem to care. To be honest, Kevia could understand it. She knew the allure that a bad boy had on a good girl because it was the same thing that attracted her to Sloan. But she had her hesitations about Polo. He was powerful and sexy, but he was dangerous too.

Licking her lips, she slid her eyes over to Star's face and then spoke once more, this time with a bit of warning in her tone.

"You know he just laid down them two dudes who was on the news. You can't handle a man like him. Them Disciple niggas ain't got it all. They too much for you."

"Oh, you can handle Sloan, but I can't handle Polo?" Star snapped, rolling her eyes.

Pressing her lips together, Kevia just shrugged. "Sloan ain't no Polo."

"You're right," Star agreed. "He ain't."

Turning back around, Star couldn't help but stare at him, caught up in a rapturous daydream about a guy that was so callous, so cruel, yet to her, he exuded a fascination that was unreal. But what Kevia said was true. Star *was* caught up, and Polo *was* crazy.

Just a while back, two armed gunmen had been found murdered, and word was that Polo was behind it. They were part of a group infamously known as the 'Four Corner Hustlers' who were in allegiance with the Disciples, rocked the same blue flag, and went to war together against the same rivals. However, two of the Four Corner Hustlers had run up in a weed spot on the block ran by a young couple that the entire hood loved and adored.

Twenty-one-year-old Fable and his nineteen-year-old fiancée, Fauna, were as real as young Black love could be. Fable went to community college at night and worked at McDonald's in the morning, while Fauna stayed home with their kids, and they sold weed on the side just for an easy come up. Everyone knew and loved them because they stayed to themselves and never caused any problems.

Needless to say, when they were murdered, the entire neighborhood was devastated; it was heartfelt. Fable and his chick were not bangin' or part of any gang. They just sold a little weed to support their family. They had two small children, girls, ages ten months and two years old. The gunmen robbed and shot up the couple, killing everything in their wake, including the two small children that had got in the way of the gunfire. The gunmen made off with only $270 and an ounce of weed.

The story made national news. A segment was even recorded for the TV show, *The First 48*. According to police, the assailants were still at large with no suspects. But only three days after the taping began for the show, two Four Corner Hustlers and a female were found in the back of an alley, hog-tied with bags over their faces and shot in the head, multiple times, execution style.

The authorities didn't know who it did but the streets did: Polo and his Disciples. The female was executed because she was the one set up the couple, Fauna's own cousin. Jealousy was a deadly disease.

"Oh shit! He's comin' this way!" Kevia gasped.

Though she didn't reply, Kevia's words weren't lost to Star, but her voice was caught up in her throat as she watched Polo take strides in her direction, still watching the streets alertly as if he was prepared for whatever. The noticeable bulge in his pants was obvious. This nigga was strapped with not just one banger but two. He was the very definition of a boss... his swag was magnificent. Walking toward her, it was like looking at God's greatest creation as his eyes roamed his surroundings, perfectly aware of everything around him. Including her.

"Damn," Star said breathlessly.

Kevia lifted one brow and looked at her, smirking slightly. She knew that her girl was really feeling Polo, and she'd picked up on the fact that he was feeling her too. Although Kevia had to admit that she'd once also fantasized about being able to grab the attention of the trap god, she always felt like Polo was untouchable and never entertained the idea that she would be able to get at him. Star, however, seemed to be exactly his type from the look in his eye whenever he saw her, but Kevia wasn't jealous. She could only be happy to be affiliated with someone who had enough pull to possibly earn his affection and all that came with it. She only hoped that whatever followed didn't lead to a bad ending.

As he walked toward them, his thick gold chain glistened in the sunlight, and Star was helpless to its hypnotic effect. Everything about him screamed money, luxury, danger, and prestige. She would be completely satisfied with the opportunity to simply bask in his light.

The two girls sat in silence, both of their stomachs jittering with nervous energy as he came closer until he was standing right in front of them, allowing them to relish in all his thug glory.

"What's good, ladies?" he chimed, his presence like catnip to kittens as the grill in his mouth sparkled. His right hand was poised on the pistol in his sagging pants as his eyes shifted over so casually like he was checking for something as he stole glances at them.

"Huh? Um, I-well... damn," Star stammered with her mouth pursed in an 'O' like she was stuck on stupid. For some reason, all Kevia did was giggle, girlishly, so much so that Polo raised an arched brow.

"Did I miss somethin'?" he asked with a penetrating stare at Star. Then his eyes lustfully traveled down from her succulent breasts to her plump, thick thighs spread out over the stair that she was seated on.

Star was suddenly conscious that her sheer cotton blue sundress had traveled up her thigh. You could see the peek-a-boo cleavage of her pink satin panties from under the lacy fabric, and Polo made sure to get more than an eye full as he licked his sexy, lubricious lips several times like he was lusting. Secretly, she liked him looking between her legs and didn't bother to cover up the exposure.

"We just getting ready for prom, looking at dresses, hoping some fiiine ass nigga will pull up on us and drop some bands full of them big face hunnids!" Kevia exclaimed and then punched Star in the arm hard, laughing hysterically at her own joke with so much glee that Star had to cut her eye at her to cool it.

Polo ignored her and continued to look at Star, then turned astutely to watch the activity on the block—every passing car, every moment, every detail, *everything*. One would get the uncanny feeling that he was watching for something specific.

Then he turned back to them and did something that completely caught Star off guard as he held on to one of the bulges in his pants. He reached over with his free hand and lightly caressed Star's thigh and grinned. He was so close that, for the first time, she saw the rose gold sparkle in the grill in his mouth as he began to speak in a sing-song mellow voice.

"Somebody has a birthday and a prom day coming up soon, huh?"

he flirted, bringing his hand back down, and she felt it scrape her inner thigh.

Star couldn't keep her composure. She bristled jovially and sat straight up on the brownstone stairs with her legs rocking with bubbling excitement that she couldn't control. Kevia, on the other hand, jumped up and pumped her fist, doing some type of hood combination of the Nae-Nae dance and a twerk, with her ass all humping in the air, hands gesturing wildly.

Star was her girl, and Kevia was just as blown away as she was to know that Polo had really been checking for her. He knew it was her birthday—that was *big* in anybody's book. Nowadays, guys didn't even remember their own mother's birthday, much-less some chick from the hood.

Star was awed by his awareness of her and couldn't help but blush as traffic passed them by, a few people curiously staring out their windows. Then she gave Kevia a stern look as she continued to dance. She was doing too much with her hyper ass.

"H-ho-how did you know I had a birthday coming up?" She couldn't help but flush red under her caramel cheeks as she lost the tug of war with her mouth, forming a big ass goofy smile.

"You 'bout to turn eighteen, shawty. Come on, man. This *my* city. This *my* spot. I know everything that goes on in this bitch."

"Wow," was all Star could mutter as she clasped her hands together in her lap, a bundle of ebullient joy. Polo really had shown interest in her! It felt like her spirit took wings and soared to the majestic heaven in the sky, taking her and Polo with it.

Then everything started happening all at once. First Kevia scoffed with her hands on her hips, talking loud enough for damn near everyone around her to hear.

"Oh, hell nah! What this hatchet-head, no edges, ugly, man-lookin' bitch lookin' at?" she spat with so much disdain that heads swiveled in her direction.

Star and Polo both followed her eyes, and there was Tonya, standing across the street looking at them with a smug expression, arms akimbo and frowning like she had just taken a bite out of something bitter. And she *had*—a bitter reality check. The love of her life,

Polo Don, was already acting like he was going to get rid of her, and to see him talking to two of the biggest hood rats that she despised more than anything on Earth, unnerved her.

She was both smoldering with irate hatred and hurt because there was also something else that troubled her deeply. From the way that Polo had been talking and acting lately, rumor was that she was about to lose her rank and her man. For her, that would be the essence of being thrown to the wolves. There was about a thousand thirsty bitches lined up that wanted her position, and two of them sat right across the street, agitating the fuck out of her.

To make matter worse, Polo started yelling about something again, loudly, and though he said no names, she got the uncanny feeling that it was about her.

"Man, fuck dat bitch! It's gon' be some serious changes around here in rank, and she know it. I'm getting ready to start demoting mutha-fuckas and promoting Gangstas and Gangstress. It's about to be a change of vanguard on some real shit."

Kevia perked up and spoke just as loudly, with confidence.

"Well, if you get rid of that bitch, I'm tryna take her place at the top, but first, lemme whoop that hoe's ass. The bitch shot me in my fuckin' leg, and I ain't never gonna forget it," she raved, pointing right at Tonya.

"Man, let that stupid shit go." Polo raised his voice and took an intimidating step toward Kevia.

Silence.

Kevia shut up real quick and pretended to toy at something on the ground with her toe. Smart move.

Tonya had looked on long enough, resisting the urge to run across the street and 'rambo' the bum-bitch Kevia with the big ass mouth. Instead, she tried a different ploy. She needed Polo to walk his ass back across the street to her and away from Star.

"Polo... Polo, baby, can I talk to you for a second? Please?" Tonya called out in a solemn voice like she was on the brink of tears as traffic passed in front of her.

Kevia and Star both glared into her. If looks could kill, she would have been massacred right there in front of the trap house.

Polo swirled, pivoting with alarming precision on his feet.

"Bitch, didn't I tell yo' fuck ass not to be calling a nigga name out like that in public?" he yelled, and the guys gambling on the side of the building all stopped and watched as if at attention. Even his crew, the foot soldiers standing out front of the trap, stood attentive. What they were really doing was letting Polo know that they were on point.

The last few years, he had been ruling with an iron fist; the stress from living in the concrete jungle was taking its toll... or he had a deadly premonition of what was to come. Whatever it was, mutha-fuckas needed to listen, or heads would roll.

It was as if a ferocious lion had roared, and its name was Polo Don, the infamous leader of the Gangsta Disciples. His intent was to keep his crew in check at all times, at all costs, especially now.

"I'm sorry, I—"

Polo dismissed her with a wave of his hand and turned around, showing her his back. Instantly, Tonya hung her head, crestfallen, and padded her royal blue sneakers across the worn pavement back to the trap house.

Like a chameleon, Polo's demeanor had suddenly changed; his jaw was clenched so tightly that Star could see the outline of his cheek-bones as he fought to keep his composure. One thing he constantly beat into the heads of anyone who knew him was to never call his name out loud in public. You never knew who could be around lurking, ready to bust a cap in his ass as soon as someone pointed him out. He was paranoid to the core, a consequence of the life he lived, but that same paranoia was what had kept him alive for so long.

Turning back to Star, he ran his hand over the bottom half of his face, glanced once more down the street, and then back to her. Licking his lips, he began to speak, his words more like a demand than a question.

"Since you'll be legal for your prom, a nigga gon' finally fuck wit' ya. I'm taking you out, so if you got some sucka ass lame nigga on deck, tell him to fall back and get ghost 'cause you gon' be with a real nigga on your birthday. You feel what I'm sayin'?"

All Star could do was tacitly nod her head like she was spellbound as she unconsciously fumbled with her hands in her lap. Her heart pounded so hard, it felt like she was hyperventilating just to breathe. It was all she could do to take in small sips of air, like she was drinking from a straw.

Then Kevia cut in, animated. "Well damn, nigga! You definitely know how to ask a bitch out on a prom date! And what you care about her bein' legal for with all the shit you do?"

Kevia's wack ass humor was going to get her killed.

Polo suddenly turned with his hand on the banger inside his pants and looked only at her for the first time. It felt like eternity. Then he cracked a smile, and it was beautiful. Star bit down on her bottom lip as she stared at the cute dimples in his cheeks. He had the kind of dimples you wanted to affectionately kiss and sink your tongue into for the rest of your life.

"I'm a model citizen. So fuck what ya heard," he joked, making them both laugh. It was a rarity, but he was in a good mood.

Overcome with excitement, Star stood, emboldened, and smoothed her tight-fitting dress down with the palm of her hands, anxious to return the love she was feeling. Despite her shyness, she was determined to give Polo a big ass hug, press her body against his, kiss his dimple, maybe even sink her tongue in there on the sly—something she had dreamed of since the day she first laid eyes on him.

But then suddenly, out of the blue, Polo lurched forward and pulled out his bangers shoving her back toward her front door.

"Yo! Yo! GD's, arms up!" he shouted, gesturing with both pistols in his hand.

Naïve in her mental fugue, she hadn't even noticed—and neither would have any normal civilian—a black Chevrolet Tahoe that Polo was clocking. It had bent the corner from nearly a block away, and although nothing seemed off about it, he had been watching it from the second it turned onto his street. He'd picked up on it even before its occupants picked up on him. Amazing feat, by any stretch of the imagination, and that may have been the reason why Polo had made it to the ripe old age of twenty-five, which was considered old for a ganglord leader on the Southside.

At Polo's cryptic signal, Disciples scattered into trained position, including a few wary dope fiends who had enough sense to get the fuck out the way. Star and Kevia dashed into her vestibule entrance of her grandmother's building and ducked down, taking cover.

Just that fast, death beckoned as mayhem threatened the torn and littered streets of the Chi, which were possibly about to be saturated with blood.

The black Tahoe came to a stop right in front of the trap house. Its four occupants hopped out with urgency, holding assault rifles in their hands. So intent on blasting up *The Spot*, neither of the gunmen saw Polo across the street with both bangers cocked, ready to initiate homicide. The would-be-assassins could have rolled right up into an ambush had not Polo been compassionate to the plight of Black life and felt the need to spare the children on the street. If not for that, their Tahoe truck would have easily been converted into a makeshift casket, a tomb for the dead.

"Yo, my nigga, what's good? Y'all pulled up in this bitch like y'all tryna touch somethin'," Polo growled with a menacing scrawl, causing the gunmen to spin around, startled.

Too late!

In the ecology of the hood, he could have easily slaughtered them. Instead, Polo was smart. He knew of the deadly consequences that would follow if he laid them down right then. That was one reasons Polo spared their lives. What also stopped him was the daunting fact that they were all young—maybe just barely in their twenties—and reckless. Years of lean and barbiturate pills had their brains numb and dumb.

Also, Polo had been expecting them.

He was standing right behind them and could have easily wet them up, which they knew as he aimed both bangers in their direction.

"We just came through to see 'bout some shit," one of them named J.B. said and lowered his assault weapon like he didn't want to get shot. J.B., the oldest at twenty, was accompanied by Assassin, Poo-Boy, and Silk.

"So that's how you niggas pull up? Holding sticks like you and your manz looking for some smoke, huh?"

Assassin decided to cut in. He was short, barely five foot five, with a serious short man complex and a big chip on his shoulder. His face was tatted; an AK-47 embellished on his right temple, a star tatted on his forehead, and crescent moon on his jaw. His light skin was freckled, and he had glistening blond curly hair like he was mixed with something.

Look at this mutt of a nigga actin' hard, Polo thought, sneering.

Assassin donned a blue bandana wrapped around his head. He spoke with grit in his tone like he had something to get off his chest. He was only eighteen-years-old, and his speech was slurred, badly. He was high off something and eager to get at Polo to show him who was boss.

"Somebody whacked Pig, J-Rock, and my girl, Shantay. From what we heard, you and the GDs was behind—"

Before Assassin's little ass could finish his sentence, Polo had pushed up on him with the quickness and whacked him twice, hard, with a vicious overhand right using his gun, and then took his pistol right out of his hand in one fluent motion.

"Oh shit!" an anonymous voice on the streets crooned.

"Damn!" both Kevia and Star exclaimed, looking through the front window with their hearts pounding with adrenaline.

They weren't the only ones peering out their vestibule window. The whole block was watching in awe.

"Nigga, Pig, J-Rock, and that bitch got bodied because they set up Fable and his girl, Fauna, and killed two small children. They got what they had comin' to them so let that shit go. Call it street justice," Polo said, breathing hard. It angered him to even have to explain this simple shit.

Just that fast, a street army of thugs, Disciples, surrounded the Tahoe truck, and the staccato of high-powered weapons being engaged with ammunition resonated with the murmur of street sounds. This was all taking place in broad daylight, but Polo this time didn't seem the least bit concerned.

Assassin was keeled over as his blood soaked the worn concrete. His buddies tried to hold their composure, suddenly realizing what they had rolled up on.

Poo-Boy was chubby with large cheeks and a fat, wobbly potbelly. In the sweltering heat, he wore a green army fatigue jacket as balls of sweat cascaded down his swollen cheeks. He licked his lips and then spoke in a voice of reasoning.

"It's just a misunderstanding, P. We was tryna figure out what happened to our people, feel me? We don't want no problems with the Gangstas." He shrugged, one hand still holding a pearl-handled .9 mm gun. "We 'posed to be on the same side. We just wanted to know what happened to our homeboys. That's all."

By his side, Silk made a noise and then wagged his head to show he was in agreement. He was the tallest one in the crew, dark as night and skinny with pop eyes and wore his long, silky hair parted in the middle, hanging long on each side. Silk was someone Polo recognized and a big part of why he was allowing them to walk away unharmed. Polo actually liked the kid and had watched him grow up from a little boy. Silk was also the son of the man who ran the Four Corner Hustlers crew, and Polo wanted to stay on good terms with him. Especially now with Mink dead and Kato down until further notice; he couldn't afford to go to war.

"Y'all young niggas drop y'all guns and head outta here. I'ma give you a pass solely on the strength y'all suppose to have an allegiance with us, but from this point on, the allegiance is over until y'all get y'all shit organized. If I ever see one of you niggas around here again, it's gon' be drama. Feel me?" Polo cut his eyes into Silk. "You make sure you let Rome know that shit," he added, referencing Silk's father.

The young goons exchanged weary glances with silent gestures but not before hesitating. The moment lulled like smoke in a bottle as they fought their inner desire to be gangsta, but in the end decided to submit to their need to survive and dropped their weapons with their faces etched in humiliation and disgrace. Assassin could barely walk because of his injuries as they all hobbled over to the truck prepared to drive away, but then Polo dropped another disgraceful bombshell on them.

"Hold up! You niggas gotta walk. We confiscating this vehicle under GD law."

"So what... you robbing us, man?" J.D. asked with a pained expression. His eyes were bloodshot red, his vanity wounded. Polo had already humiliated them in the worst way.

"Nigga, if I was robbin' you, I would take your life. I'm letting you walk away, so consider yourself lucky."

"But we got a bunch of money and dope in the truck from a lick we just hit!" J.B. said with a hint of plea in his voice and then reached his hand toward the vehicle like he was going to retrieve it.

Before he could move another muscle, Polo aimed the Desert Eagle in his hand at J.B.'s head, causing him to flinch in fear.

"Well, thanks for the donation, nigga." Polo chuckled maliciously. "Now get the fuck up outta here. I'm counting to three, and then we using y'all niggas for target practice. Just like your people did Fable and his girl."

Not wanting to call his bluff, they all took off running, and Polo's crew got a good laugh out of that. Everybody except Polo.

His gut-wrenching feeling was telling him he would see their faces again, and it wouldn't be good. He had just committed a cardinal sin. *You never pull a gun on a man and not use it*. That law was written by the Hoover himself and was a rule he lived by. Going against that shit would come back to bite you in the ass every single time.

Inside the vestibule, Star and Kevia were filled with apprehension and riveting suspense. The entire time, it felt like Star had been holding her breath. Her heart was racing as she watched Polo put in work. He wasn't even hers yet, but she felt the muscle swelling with pride as if he already was. The place between her legs was moist and hotter than it had ever been before. If she thought she had wanted him before, it was nothing in comparison to the desire she felt now.

She and Kevia both knew the young Four Corner Hustlers, *all* of them. The one by the name of Assassin, had once bought a gun to class and then had eventually been kicked out for fights. Silk seemed to have a crush on Star and had stepped to her plenty of times, but she never gave him any play, thinking that he was a lame trying to play a gangsta. Everyone knew who his father was, and because of Rome's reputation, Silk thought he was a boss. But it was obvious to anyone who laid eyes on him that he was a pretender, definitely not cut out for the street life, as evidenced by how everything went down only a few moments before.

"Damn, that nigga is more legit than I even thought." Kevia

gushed, speaking the words that matched Star's thoughts. "He knocked Assassin in his shit, stole his gun, took the whip, *and* made them niggas have to catch the bus back home. He's *sick as hell!*"

"Mm hmm," Star agreed, smiling a little to herself. Her young heart was there for Polo to take. She couldn't wait until prom night arrived.

CHAPTER 8

PEAKING OUT OF THE BENT-UP BLINDS ON HER BEDROOM WINDOW, Star couldn't contain her excitement as she waited for Polo to arrive. Not a soul other than Kevia knew who would be accompanying her to prom, and that was exactly how she wanted it. Once she burst through the door of the school's auditorium on the arm of the most sought-after nigga in all of the Chi, that would be a statement enough for them all. Her nerves were frazzled, her stomach was twisted in knots—she felt like she would faint from sheer anticipation. Running over to her dresser, she peered into the small, cracked mirror there for about the hundredth time, checking her makeup and hair. She was flawless but couldn't help fussing over the long tresses that she'd flat-ironed bone straight, letting them flow down her back.

I'ma be stuntin' on them hoes, Star thought as she applied another layer of strawberry lip gloss over her lips, admiring the way the gloss made them pop. She was still nervous as ever. On the edge of her dresser was a partial blunt. She fired it up to quell her nerves as she listened to her mother and grandma argue through the thin wall. Something about missing rent money that Roxy claimed to have lost.

Star quickly tossed the banter of outside noises out her brain and mellowed as smoke curled from her nostrils. She admired her figure in the mirror—her breasts, her ass. If things went her way, Polo would be getting it all later on tonight.

As luck would have it, prom fell on her birthday, but instead of expecting gifts, this year, she wanted to give one. At eighteen-years-old, Star was a virgin—not by choice but by circumstance. She'd never met a boy that she was feeling enough to give her body to, but all that would change soon because tonight, she would be in the presence of a grown man. Tonight would be the night that her dreams were made of. For as long as she could remember, she'd been making love to Polo with her mind, but now she would have the chance to put in action everything that she'd only been able to experience in her mind.

Her phone chirped, and her body tensed as a jolt of electricity shot up through her spine and the blunt burnt her fingers. She tossed it like a hot potato and ran to grab the phone, hoping that it was Polo saying that he was on his way. She was only mildly disappointed to see that it wasn't him but Kevia who had texted instead.

Biiiiiitttch, I'm too hype! You ready?

Star laughed before pecking out her reply. Kevia was already on one, she could tell. Probably had already started on her pre-game and taken a few shots to get her mood right.

I can't wait! Your cousin got the room?

Hell yeah! was Kevia's reply. *You just better remember to call my ass in the morning and tell me everything that happened. I want all dick details!*

A sound somewhere between a snort and a giggle escaped from Star's nostrils, and she rolled her eyes, smiling. Kevia was not only crazy but nosy as hell. But it was the right of a best friend to hear all the explicit details of a girl's first time, and Star wouldn't rob her of that.

You know I will, Star promised before placing the phone down.

She heard a light knock on her door and rolled her eyes, hoping that it wasn't Roxy coming to beg for money, especially since the rent money was missing again, and Star knew she would have to pay it with money she had saved. The past few weeks, it was no secret that she was earning a little something by doing makeup and hair, but she had to find creative ways to hide her cash whenever she wasn't around. Roxy could pick up the scent of money like a bloodhound and had already found her stash on plenty of occasions in the past, just like Roxy was able to do to her granny. She had to be more careful if she didn't want to get caught slipping again.

"Who is it?" Star asked with a terse tone as she quickly sprayed the room with perfume. Everything about this night had to go perfectly. The last thing she wanted was for Roxy to come by spoiling things before they even got a chance to get started.

"It's me," Ebony's tiny voice said from the other side. "I wanna see your dress!"

Rushing over, Star quickly fanned the thin bellows of smoke and unlocked the door and pulled it open, tugging Ebony inside the room by her arm before closing the door behind her. As soon as she was able to collect herself enough to really look at her older sister, Ebony's eyes filled with tears, and she covered her mouth with her hand as she took her in. Star had always been more of a tomboy than a girly girl, so seeing her all dressed up like a model who could grace the pages of a high fashion magazine was a treat that Ebony had not been expecting.

"You're so pretty!" Ebony squealed, and both girls jumped up and down, giggling with childish excitement. Then suddenly, Ebony's eyes dimmed just a bit as she dropped her tone and asked a question.

"Are you still goin' with Polo?"

"Hell yeah!" Star shot back, cocking her neck to the side as if to ask whether Ebony had lost her mind. "Why wouldn't I? He asked me, and I damn sure wasn't about to say no to the one nigga in the city who could be with any woman he chooses."

Licking her lips, Ebony's eyes cut a little to the side, and she paused for a beat before continuing. She wasn't attracted to the allure of a gangsta like so many other girls in the hood, her own sister included.

"I know but... he's just kinda scary, ain't he?"

Shaking her head, Star rolled her eyes at her younger sister. Ebony just didn't get it. She wasn't the type of girl that was caught up in a thug's appeal the way that Star was. Innocent, sheltered, and more than a little bit of a nerd, Ebony preferred the good ole boys: geeks and brainiacs who preferred to spend their weekends in the library studying rather than running from block-to-block. Which was cool for her, but Star wanted something a bit different. There was nothing that a nerd ass dude could do for her but show her where to find a *real* man.

"He's not scary... He's respected," Star told her with her nose in the air and a smug look on her face. "There is a difference. You'll learn when you're grown."

Smiling, Ebony rolled her eyes. "And you're grown now?"

"I will be tonight," Star said, a smile teasing the edges of her lips.

Ebony wasn't too young not to catch her meaning, and her eyes widened, rounding off into full circles.

"You're not talking about what I think you're talking about, right?"

Before Star could get a chance to answer, her phone chimed, and she grabbed it quickly, knowing in her heart that this was the moment she'd been waiting for. As soon as she looked at the screen and saw that she had a message from Polo, the flutters returned to her stomach, and she rushed to read his message.

I'm outside.

"He's here!"

Reaching out, Ebony grabbed her sister and hugged her tight. "Have fun!"

Pulling away, she took one more look at Star and couldn't help but think about her own prom, even though she'd never before even considered attending any school dances. To her, they seemed silly—a waste of money and a waste of time. People did *the most* when it came to prom, hatching all these extravagant plans to please the same people you saw every single day. It just made no sense.

But looking at the excitement in Star's eyes had her fantasizing about things she'd never wanted before. All her life, Ebony looked up to her older sister and copied damn near everything she did, so this moment wasn't any different. Not to mention, Star was drop-dead gorgeous with her body popping, her makeup on fleek, and her hair silky straight, showing off her length. She couldn't be any more beautiful than she was right now if she tried.

Grabbing her clutch, Star gave her sister one last slick smile and then took off in a confident strut out of her room, heading straight to the front door. If things went the way she wanted, as soon as Polo saw her, he would fall in love. It didn't matter if he had a girl. Tonya was a non-factor, and Star would do everything possible to make sure she continued to be that.

Or at least I will try, she told herself.

"Girl, look at you!"

Before she could get to the door, Star heard Geraldine coming up behind her, and turned, smiling brightly at the look in her grandmother's eyes. Behind her stood Roxy, and she was looking at Star from head-to-toe, her arms folded tight across her chest.

"How do I look?" Star asked, twirling around to give them both a better look.

"You look like new money," Geraldine gushed, grinning hard at her granddaughter. She pulled the oxygen mask from her face and walked over to kiss Star lightly on her cheek.

"Yeah, new money is right," Roxy added. "How the hell you afford all of this?"

Leave it to Roxy to pocket-watch instead of complimenting her own daughter on such a monumental day. If anything, Roxy was consistent in all ways, so it wasn't like Star could really be surprised. When it came to all things in life, Roxy only seemed to be worried about herself, and this moment wasn't any different. Rolling her eyes at her mother, Star didn't answer and instead kissed Geraldine goodbye.

"Don't wait up," was the last thing she said before she walked out the door, wanting to leave before Roxy got a chance to stop her with more questions.

OPENING THE DOOR, the crisp Chicago air was refreshing as the stars danced in the dark sky. It was the perfect setting for the perfect day. Star walked out, careful not to trip in her stiletto heels, keeping her neck bent to survey the ground ahead of her. When she finally lifted her eyes, the first vision in front of her was Polo looking like something straight off the pages of a magazine.

Damn.

Leaning against the door of what appeared to be a brand-new Maybach, it was obvious that he'd spared no expense for this night. He wasn't the type of nigga to wear a suit, but he didn't have to. Dressed from top to bottom in Gucci, his brand of choice, with his wrist, ears, and neck dripping with platinum and diamonds, he was shining like a star. Just being in his presence made her feel like a celebrity. She felt giddy, which seemed a little childish, but she couldn't bridle her excitement.

There was just one problem: there were two other cars with him, a Dodge Charger and a Chevy Caprice. Star had forgotten that going out with a young, prized gangsta came with a price—he was always with his henchmen for security purposes. Rarely was he alone.

"You look good as fuck," he said in a low tone as he allowed his eyes to drape over her luscious figure. His approval showed on his face, and she relished in his attention.

Smiling hard, Star lifted her hands up and turned around slowly, giving her ass a subtle wiggle to make sure that it caught his focus. By the time she turned back around, he was licking his juicy lips and rubbing his hands together. This was the exact response she'd hoped for. His long dreadlocks were pulled back in a sexy style, reminding her of the rapper Future, except that Polo was covered head-to-toe in tattoos.

"Thank you," she purred, feeling extra juiced by the way that he couldn't seem to tear his eyes from her thick frame. Everything she'd bought for this night had cost a grip, but she wouldn't hesitate to do it all again just to see that look in his eyes.

"Damn, Polo, that's you?" a man walking down the sidewalk asked. The sight of her stopped him right in his tracks.

In fact, as Star looked around her, she noticed that all eyes were on her, including Polo's henchmen. Everyone was amazed that the same girl who had grown up on the block, fighting at the drop of a dime, smoking weed, and talking shit was able to switch her style up so suddenly. To them, it was almost like a magic trick, but to Star, it was a much-needed ego boost.

"Yeah, this all me, nigga, so close yo' fuckin' mouth and keep walkin'," Polo replied, gritting on the man until he got the message. One of his men in the car laughed, and Star couldn't help but smirk.

I'm all his! She was over the moon.

Her stomach was jittering with butterflies. The night was already off to a wonderful start, but little did she know... this was only the beginning.

"WHAT THE FUCK YOU LOOKIN' nervous for?" Polo asked, chuckling a little as he adjusted something on his waist.

Instantly, she thought she knew what it was and prayed it wasn't. As they walked toward the car, she honestly thought there was a chance Polo would run around the other side and open the door for her. She even slowed her pace. It never happened. He hopped his ass in the car and looked at her like she was crazy for walking so slow.

Can't have it all, she thought with a subtle shrug as she opened her own door and stepped in.

CHAPTER 9

PULLING UP TO ENGLEWOOD HIGH, ALL EYES WERE ON THEM AS they filed in followed by a small caravan of cars. Although prom had already started, there was still a crowd of people outside, and it seemed like as soon as they saw Polo's Maybach approaching the building, all conversations came to a stop. There was only one nigga in the hood who could afford a ride this fly, so it was obvious that Polo was on the scene, but the question in all of their eyes was, *who* was the girl he was with? Who could possibly be lucky enough to have the trap god personally escorting her to her senior prom?

"I don't know if I can do this," Star whispered, losing her nerves all of a sudden. It was crazy how she had wanted the attention and even dreamed of it, but now that it was here, she was second-guessing herself.

"Aye," Polo called out to her, reaching out to lightly touch her face and nudge her so that she was looking at him. "You're rolling with a boss, so all that nervous shit gotta go. You sexy as fuck, and ain't no bitch in here gon' be able to come next to matching your fly big booty ass." He squeezed her thigh with his rough hand, and she felt her clitoris jump.

"Okay. Lemme catch my breath," she said with giddiness and fanned her moist brow with her hand.

"Damn, yo' ass over there sweating and shit for real. You nervous as fuck, huh?"

"Look at all them lookin' at us." Nervously, her voice raised a notch.

"Yeah, 'cause you fuckin' with a real nigga! Polo Don off up in this bitch, and you too. This the lifestyle of a trill nigga, so suck that shit up and get used to it. Be about it or be without it... or you want me to drop you back at the crib?"

She reached out and grabbed his hand in hers and squeezed it tight like she was sinking in water and he was her lifesaver.

"Hell no! I wanna be with you tonight and every night... Whatever you want," she said. Her bottom lip trembled slightly, and she had a flashback of her dreams of him and felt a familiar shiver between her thighs.

With a half-smirk, Polo replied, "Now that's what the fuck I'm talkin' about. I knew you had some gangsta in you. You need to wear that shit, *believe* that shit. That's where you'll get your confidence. Feed off my energy. Do I look like I give a fuck 'bout another nigga?" He snarled slightly and adjusted something in his waist again. She cast a glance down, and there was a big ass chrome-plated .9 mm tucked in his waistband.

Pressing her lips together, Star tried her best to smile as she shook her head. It was hard. In reality, she was still nervous as fuck.

"That's muthafuckin' right," he quipped with the diamond grill in his mouth sparkling in the dim hue of the car like a luminous chandelier. The entire time, students did their best to gawk inside the exotic car, trying to get a better look inside.

Suddenly, Polo's phone rang, and the sound was coming from the speakers in the car. He pushed a bottom on the steering wheel as he checked his rearview mirror.

"Yo, what's good?" Polo asked and looked over at Star. She played it off and acted like she saw someone interesting out the window, and actually, she did. Taylor Smith, the nerdy ass white boy that tried to act black in school, was trying to see through the dark tints in her window. He was in her science class, smart as fuck and liked black girls, especially her, a lot.

"Lisa, the Gangstress under Tonya found Tommy Gun on the 'Gram. He tryin' to smash. She waiting for him to call back. If he do and she set up the meet, what you want us to do?" the voice asked on the interior speaker phone.

Polo flinched with obvious anger. "Punish that nigga, but first make sure the nigga got the product that he ran off with. Knowing his hustling ass, he probably done reupped with more. Make him tell us where it's at once you get him. Make sure to drop him on his grandma's front porch. We gotta make an example outta niggas that steal from us. And..."

The fury in Polo's voice was undeniable before he suddenly stopped talking. His words trailed off as he realized that he was talking too much. Star pull down the sun visor and pretended like she was checking her makeup, but she could feel his eyes boring into her skull. Her hands were trembling.

"My nigga, hit me back if y'all get him. I can't talk right now."

"Bet," the voice on the other end responded.

After a few moments of tense silence, Polo turned to Star and asked, "You ready?"

All she could do was tactfully nod her head yes. He could see her hands shaking and inwardly cursed himself for even having that conversation in front of her. She was a Gangstress, but still, that wasn't something he wanted her to overhear just yet.

In an effort to calm her nerves, he leaned over and pressed his lips against hers, shocking her to the max.

Kissing Polo wasn't like anything she had ever experienced before. For someone with a body so hard and ripped with divinely crafted muscles, his lips were soft and inviting. Star quickly lost herself in the moment. Channeling his aggression, she deepened the kiss and sucked hard on his lips as if half the school wasn't standing there watching. She became a vixen—taking complete control of the moment and even surprised her damn self by adding some tongue into the mix.

She's dope as fuck, Polo thought to himself, loving the way she was opening up to him. She was making the job easy for him. He needed to gain her trust, and he needed to gain it quickly. Once she trusted him, it was only a short journey from there to her heart.

It was the end of the school year, and word was that Star was trying to be on the first thing smoking out the hood. He couldn't have that. Although Polo hadn't spent much time with her one-on-one, his eyes were trained enough to pick up on her inner-strength, even if she hadn't seen it in herself. He needed that type of strength on his team. He needed her in his life. There were things about Star that Polo knew which she didn't even know about herself, and those things only made her even more of a trophy in his mind. She was the daughter of the most respected Black Gangsta alive, outside of himself.

There was only one thing that consistently plagued his mind, and he tried not to think on it, but it was hard. It was still unsettling to think that she may have played a part in his brother's death—even more troubling to know that she'd even seen him die—but he didn't want to spend too much time on that, because doing so meant that he couldn't have her.

There was something about the light of a good girl that connected with the darkness in a street nigga's heart, and it was no different with Polo and Star. She was too good for him to pass up. A smart girl; pure innocence hidden under the cloak of the right amount of savage and sass. Then there was this kiss... After only one taste of her lips, Tonya immediately became a non-factor. He would never want her again.

"You better chill on that shit before a nigga make a move and give you something you can't handle..." Polo said with a crooked smile, testing the waters.

He suspected she was a virgin, but he had to be sure. That was the only type of woman that he deemed worthy enough to spend his time with and stake claim on. Like any nigga of his stature, he'd fucked more than his share of thots, but only a chick that was pure and untouched could sit next to him on his throne.

"I can handle anything and everything you wanna give me," Star replied cockily, licking her lips for good measure.

Polo's brow lifted. "Yeah? So you be out here driving these niggas crazy, huh?"

Star felt her cheeks flame. No one knew she was a virgin, not even Kevia.

Two summers ago, Star lied and told Kevia that a boy named Travis had popped her cherry after she revealed that she had lost her virginity to Sloan. The lie could have easily been verified, but Travis was gunned down in the middle of the streets less than a week later.

It was a freak accident, gang-related, but he wasn't even involved; just got caught in the crosshairs of war between the Vice Lords and Black Gangstas while minding his business on the way to the mall. It was then that Star realized that it didn't matter who you are or how good you were, the streets respected no one, and a bullet didn't have any names on it. Anyone could catch a hot ball at any time if you were in the wrong place at the wrong time.

"I've been told a few times that I know how to do my thing," Star lied, bragging while licking her lips and forcing confidence that she didn't have. She was hit with a brush of anxiety but tried not to falter in her sex appeal. On the inside, however, her mind was reeling. She was laying it on thick to be someone who had no idea if she could really deliver.

"Is that right?" Polo asked, but he'd already lost some interest.

He was disappointed to know that he'd been wrong about Star, but it was all good. He might not be able to make her his main woman, but they could at least have fun for the night, especially since it was her birthday too, before he curbed her for good.

Pushing her out of the part of his mind he initially had her in, he decided to swap up his style and treat her like he did any other chick he only wanted to entertain for the night. The allure she once had was gone.

PROM WAS a dream other than the fact that Polo was being shadowed by his henchmen. But even that added to his thug allure. Girls were hitting on his men; they were stealing the attention from the young boys at Star's school. Most of the time, Polo stayed posted up on the wall with his back against it and smiled, to Star's delight, as she danced, rubbing her ass against him and twerking so hard that her dress would come up, exposing her sexy thick thighs. Star's feet were killing her in the stiletto high heels, but you wouldn't know it from how she was putting on a show, making Polo grin like he was watching a porn show. Occasionally, she even saw him have to adjust himself.

Then came the drama.

Taylor Smith strolled his ass up nonchalantly and stood in front of Polo, blocking his view. He had corn-colored silk hair and thick bifocals. The black tuxedo he had on looked ancient and was about two sizes too big. However, at six foot four, 240 pounds, Taylor could be intimidating to some.

"Hey, Star. I been peeping you dancing and shit. Can I have a dance—"

Wham!

Before he could finish his sentence, Polo had yoked him barehanded around his neck and slammed him against the wall so hard that Taylor's glasses flew across the dancefloor, and his hair feathered in front of his face, completely blinding him.

"I know muthafuckin' well your white ass saw me standing here!" Polo raged through his teeth, his voice low but so cold that it seemed like he was yelling at the same time. He pulled his fist back like he was about to punch him, but he didn't have to. Within seconds, his crew was on the white boy, prepared to give him a serious beatdown.

Star managed to scurry between the two of them, trying to incite peace amidst the chaos.

"Polo, he don't know any better! He's not from our hood... He's slow if it don't have nothing to do with school," she pleaded, but it was too late. One of Polo's henchmen reached back and slugged the shit out the white boy, causing his head to hit the brick wall.

"Stop it!" Star raised her voice just as a couple of students took notice. A few teachers started moving their way, and Star began to panic.

"Chill out!" Polo gestured with his arms to his crew and took a second look at Taylor. He hadn't even attempted to fight back. His face was beet red, hair askew.

"Dude, I'm sorry!" Taylor huffed seeming out of breath.

It looked like his eyes were rolling around in his head; he was punch drunk. Just then, one of the school's security guards walked up. He was a white off-duty police officer with an attitude. Star looked at Polo, and she could clearly see the bulge of the pistol in his pants.

Things were going from bad to worse.

"Is everything okay over here?" the cop asked, looking around suspiciously, then focused his attention on Taylor. Even though he was dressed in civilian clothes, a suit and tie for the occasion, everybody knew he was a cop.

Time stalled like tight tension on a thin rope as Taylor's mouth moved without words, and he finally said, "These are my buddies. We having a good time. It's prom night. You can move on." He then playfully punched Polo on the shoulder.

The entire time, Star had her eyes closed, pinched tight. When she opened them to watch the cop walk off, she noticed one of Polo's men had his hand inside his jacket on his strap.

Star didn't care what anybody said. From then on, she had newfound respect for Taylor, and so did Polo. He dapped up the awkwardly dressed white boy as the entire crew exchanged words, including Sloan.

As Taylor walked off to ask another Black girl for a dance, everyone seemed at ease, but no one was as much as Star. Dating a young hoodlum gangsta like Polo wasn't going to be easy, but if given the chance, she would eagerly welcome the challenge.

And just that fast, things were back to normal. A song by Cardi B. came on, and Star once again began to wind her ass without missing a beat, making Polo smile like a Cheshire Cat as he leaned back against the wall. Out of the blue, Kevia popped up from nowhere, decked out and looking fly with a long, flowing Prada dress, matching accessories, shoes, purse, and expensive hair weave. She giddily spoke to Polo, and for some reason he frowned, giving her a subtle nod of his head before mumbling "'Sup?"

She was hype as she danced right next to Star.

"What's been goin' on? He tried to get some ass yet?" she asked, swaying off-beat with a red plastic party cup in her hand.

"Girl, hush. You're loud!" Star retorted comically, and together they fell into each other, laughing hilariously like the two school girls they were. In this moment, the harsh world that was their normal life didn't exist. It was prom night.

"I'll tell you later. Bye!" Star teased and shoved Kevia, but she didn't budge. Instead, she thrust the red cup in Star's face.

"Drink this. It'll make you ride that dick like a cowgirl." Kevia giggled and staggered slightly. She was still moving her thin hips off beat to the music.

Sniffing the contents, Star peered inside the cup, hesitated, then took a big gulp. It tasted strong but delicious. Some of the liquor even dribbled down her chin, but she licked at it with her tongue. Pure ambrosia!

Star sucked her lips and danced, her eyebrows bent in an inquisitive expression that her girl Kevia knew all too well. She rolled her eyes hard and decided to go ahead and explain herself.

"Bitch, it's only Peach Patrón, and you know it's too good to be all that strong, so don't trip. You can keep the cup, too. We got a whole half a gallon bottle stashed in the bathroom," Kevia sang then turned around and strutted her ass over to a group of girls she hung with but Star only tolerated. Instead of following after her, Star took a glance back at Polo.

As soon as she turned around, she saw something in his eyes—or maybe it was the large gulp of Patrón she had just swallowed—but whatever it was, love or lust, it set her sex on fire. He was watching her intently, and it made her just bold enough to dance over to him, ever so sensually, and grind her body against his as they continued to make eye contact. It was something that felt natural and primitive.

When he reached out to palm both her ass cheeks, it felt like she melted in his hands. She happened to notice people watching, but she loved the attention. She was on stage, sort of like when she posted a picture on the 'Gram and would get twenty thousand likes in no time. She loved it. With insatiable desire, she cavorted and turned around, bending over before pressing up close onto him, rubbing her ass against his lap like it was on fire with fervid heat.

Star couldn't help but hear the ruckus yelling from a distance. It sounded like Kevia applauding and laughing, all animated, as if Star was on stage performing a striptease.

Star stole a glance over her shoulder and was surprised to see Polo with such a large grin as he leaned forward and grabbed her hips, pressing his torso hard against her with a serious 'I want to dick you down' scowl on his face. She suddenly felt something stiff and long in his pants.

It had to be his gun. Or was it?

Before she knew it, she had deepened her grind, pressing her ass against the huge bulge in his pants. It blew her mind when she felt Polo pushing back, matching her fevered passion. They were playing fuck games, child's play with a very grown-up ending that Star may have not been prepared for.

Then it happened.

With the music blaring in their ears, a slow and melodic sound-track to their lust, there right on the dance floor, their bodies created a rhythm of impromptu dry fucking. Star noticed several of her friends gawking with jovial grins and bashful smiles of teenage glee, including Kevia, the ringleader. Star continued on, as if the world was their stage, oblivious to everyone.

"Fuck Tonya," he whispered, and she laughed out loud, somewhat taken aback by his sudden proclamation, and took a long sip from her cup.

I dreamed about this, she thought, smiling.

The tempo of the music sped up as another song began, breaking their flow. Star began to notice Polo peeking at his phone a few times, checking his incoming texts. Her jealousy was quick and intense, forming a small knot in her chest as he glanced at it once more, the ambient blue light glowing on his handsome face.

Star pursed her lips, pouting silently while cutting her eyes up at him. Was it Tonya texting him? She pressed her backside hard against him, trying to steal his attention.

With stern capriciousness, he pushed off her and spoke above the music with a slight snarl.

"Yo, ma, hold up a sec." This time, he gave her a softer nudge away with the tips of his fingers as his eyes scrolled around the auditorium.

She turned and rose to her tiptoes, a futile attempt to reach his towering height and make eye contact again. Star was good at reading people's body language, and her better judgement told her something was up, so she gave him a subtle nod, something that conveyed she understood, and tactfully danced over to a group of girls, including Kevia, who had been anxiously watching and waiting for her company.

Instantly, like hyperactive teenagers, as soon as Star entered the fray with the other girls, they all started screaming and yelling, jumping up and down—wildin' out, or so it appeared—but Star kept a curious eye on Polo as he spoke to his men, hoping everything was alright.

It wasn't.

Sloan and Polo and his GD of henchmen walked over near the men's restroom and began to talk off to the side when, once again, the white undercover security cop strolled by. He tried to act nonchalant, but it was obvious he was attempting to ear hustle, trying to pick up on the conversation. Noting that they were being watched, Polo ran his hand over his low-cut goatee and turned to Sloan just as the security officer strode by.

"Shit, they up to somethin'," Star muttered under her breath.

"Girl, did I hear you say, 'pour something'?" Kevia asked excitedly, while bouncing around on her feet.

Sucking her teeth, Star just sighed and rolled her eyes before giggling and following Kevia to the bathroom. She could use a refill of the Patrón.

"I JUST WANTED all the folks on point. Don't nobody turn around, but it's about ten or fourteen of them Four Corner Hustlers off in this bitch, and I think they packin'. One of them is Assassin, the nigga you gave the beat down to," Sloan said with a stiff top lip, his brow creased in deep indignation. The tension was so thick you could cut it with a butter knife.

"Where?" was all Polo asked and eased his hand into his waistband onto one of the straps he was carrying.

"Over all the way in the back. By the bleachers." Sloan gestured, nodding, while casually pointing them out with his head.

"Damn, them niggas thick back there. They must be on some ambush shit, so we gon' get them first with some element of surprise shit," Polo said with grit, his mind churning.

He was a strategic master at gorilla warfare. He also welcomed murder when he deemed it necessary. A challenge in a kill or be killed environment was that there were no alternatives and no ultimatums, regardless of the fact the place was filled, jammed-pack with jubilant, hyperactive young teenagers that only came to celebrate a new period in their pre-adult journey. In this case, he had no choice.

"Y'all walk counter-clockwise, and me and Forte gon' dodge behind the bleachers and creep up from the blindside. If them niggas even flinch, wet they ass up!" Polo commanded with authority.

"What about the off-duty cop?" Forte, his third in command, asked.

"He can get it too. My job is to take my team out of here, even if it means a blood bath and a nosy ass cop getting slumped. Now move out!"

THE PLAN, a subterfuge, worked. Assassin and his crew watched Sloan and the GD's approaching and started murmuring amongst themselves.

"There them fuck niggas go. But where is that bitch ass nigga, Polo?" Assassin said all antsy with his hand on his banger. He was on the brink of hysteria as he craned his neck, looking around. He was already high off Molly and paranoid after ingesting a large amount of Percocet and Lean.

Polo moved stealthily from the rear behind Assassin and his goons, completely out of sight. They were able to sneak in through a side door entrance.

Assassin was unnerved. He wasn't trying to start a war with the Gangstas—maybe at some point in the near future, but not right now. He no longer attended the school but his sister was graduating that year and had invited him to celebrate with her at prom with some of his boys. Assassin and his crew just came to holla at some females and show his sister some love. By happenstance, Polo showed up with the Gangstas.

Still recovering from Polo's attack over a week back, he looked like an opossum in the face with two bruised black eyes and a half-mended fractured nose bent and pushed to the side. Anxiously, he wagged his head from side-to-side, looking for Polo.

"Yo, what's poppin'? Y'all niggas look like somethin' 'bout to jump off," Sloan said with a clenched jaw.

His voice had an icy tone filled with deadly intent. Cuffed in his right hand was a fifteen shot .9 mm with enough bullets to accommodate a party of ten to fourteen. The gun was leveled at Assassin's chest.

"Nigga, you don't see us in this bitch fifteen deep? We packing AK's, AR-15's, and sawed offs in this bitch. So I suggest you put dat little ass gun down." Assassin spoke with confidence he didn't really have, but the drugs had him on a suicide mission.

Polo moved stealthily from the rear behind Assassin and his goons, out of sight, and eased up right behind Assassin, so close that when he spoke, Assassin could feel Polo's breath on the back of his neck. He nearly shit in his pants. Immediately, his mind had flashbacks of the ass whipping he had received a week ago.

"Or what?" Polo challenged.

The .44 Desert Eagle was pointed in Assassin's back so tight that he felt the barrel digging into his skin; for some reason, it felt like a hot iron. The anticipation of getting shot was enough to make his high wear off.

"M—Man, y'all came up in here with dat bullshit," Assassin said with a pang of apprehension and dread as all his crew slowly turned. Forte had them covered with M4 Carbine, small and compact. It was a lethal weapon that could shoot a hundred rounds per second.

"Any of you niggas move and I'ma start spraying wit' dis bitch, massacre style. Might get you fuck niggaz on the news for yo' mama to see," was all Forte had to say. His resume was impeccable and his street cred was on one hundred, second only to Kato, his mentor.

The Four Corner Hustlers froze like mannequins in a store front and with good reason.

"Po... Po—Polo, man, what you doin'? We ain't even fuckin' wit' y'all this time," Assassin said in a whiny voice devoid of any masculinity.

"I'm about to push your wig back, nigga. Game over. I told you not to fuck with me!" Polo raged and cocked the gun, about to squeeze on Assassin to make a much-needed example of him.

"For what, mane? My sister here! This her prom night. We wasn't even thinking about y'all. That's her over there dancing with Kevia and them."

"Stop lying." Polo raised his voice, prepared to handle his business.

"Man, I put that on God!" Assassin's voice had a deep cadence like a pensive sob was in his throat about to erupt.

Polo was about to pull the trigger, knowing his crew would follow his lead. Once they did, it would sound like the Fourth of July in the packed auditorium with sparks flying and all.

Sloan stopped him in a nick of time.

"Hold up!" Sloan raised his voice so loud, several patrons in the facility turned their heads in their direction.

"He ain't lying. That *is* his sister, now that I think of it. In fact, Kevia and his sister snuck in a bottle of Patrón. I was the one who bought it for them at the store."

For some reason, Sloan's heart was racing as Polo looked between him and Assassin. Sloan knew Polo all too well. He still wanted to kill Assassin and his entire crew. That was just how Polo thought and was the reason he reached his position at such a young age.

Just then, the off-duty cop started walking toward them but Polo peeped the move.

"GDs, fall back," Polo ordered and took a seat next to Assassin, who by then was sweating profusely.

They all sat and watched the cop stroll by. Unbeknownst to him, he had been three seconds from being shot execution style.

As soon as the cop passed, Polo was the first to speak, and his words shocked everyone, maybe even including himself.

"Dig, my nigga. I thought you was on one, so me and the folks had to pull up, thinking y'all niggas wanted some smoke. But seeing that it is your sister's prom night, and on the strength that I want to move forward not backwards, we got a truce. No more killin', especially not with your sister in the building. We want her to make it to college, right?" Polo asked with a subtle threat that was enough to make Assassin's eyebrows knot in recognition of what was really being conveyed.

"Ye—yeah, w—we good, we good," Assassin stammered as he mopped at his brow with the back of his hand and continued to keep his eye on Polo.

What he didn't realize was that Polo was fighting off competing thoughts in his mind. Once again, he had violated a sacred law and pulled a gun out on a man without using it.

He was guilty of doing this *twice*, and as luck would have it, with the same nigga.

POLO and his boys began to mob back over toward Star's direction. She had been watching them intently, certain there was drama in the air, especially when she noticed the off-duty cop walk over.

Suddenly, Kevia nudged her with a sharp elbow, snapping her out of her reverie. Star's mind was all over the place when Kevia said with her breath smelling like booze, "You got every bitch in here lookin' at you crazy. You know you done made a lot of enemies, right?"

Star already knew that what Kevia was saying was more than true. Her attention had been on Polo and the gang. However, it was no secret since the moment she walked into the auditorium, with Polo by her side, she'd been getting hit with looks of admiration, awe, or pure jealousy.

There wasn't a girl in the hood who hadn't at some point fantasized about being the woman in Polo's life, and the fact that he was finally showing interest in someone other than Tonya, and it was Star of all people, had all the hatin' ass hoes on fire. She was supposed to be the mutt of the hood, the one girl who everybody talked shit about because she wasn't pressed about getting their approval on anything she chose to do. But over night, it was like the ugly duckling had turned into a beautiful swan and was grabbing up everything they always wanted but could never get.

"I'm not worried about these hoes. Not even Brenda's hatin' ass,"

Star said, cutting her eyes to Tonya's best friend, who had been staring holes in her head the entire night.

If looks could kill, Star would be six feet under with Brenda stomping on her casket to send it down a few feet further. Her eyes were like lasers, and no matter where Star turned or what she did, Brenda and her bird-brain crew of pigeons were watching. Still, she wasn't crazy enough to do shit. Star had walked in with Polo, meaning that she'd pulled rank in a way they'd never thought she could. There wasn't a damn thing any of them could do about it.

"You heard the news, right?" Kevia said, all excited with her eyes lit up with the kind of excitement that came right before tea was spilled. "About Tonya."

Frowning slightly, Star turned her way and shook her head.

"It looks like Polo is really about to kick her ass to the curb!" She began to laugh, tossing her head backward as Star only stared with wide eyes, not believing what she was hearing.

"He 'bout to whaaaat?"

Recovering from her giddy laughter, Kevia pushed her face close to Star's, nearly nose-to-nose, and spoke slowly and clearly so she could understand every word coming from her mouth.

"He... 'bout to... kick... her... ass... *out!* I heard from Renee that Tonya been livin' with Brenda and Kush the past few days. That's probably why that hoe over there lookin' at you like that. It might not even be about you bein' with Polo. She probably mad that after seeing y'all together, it seems old girl 'bout to be posted up at her crib longer than she thought!"

"Damn..." Star said, half-smiling as she thought all that through.

If Polo was really about to be done with Tonya and was showing her off in public, claiming her as his, she might actually have a chance at taking her place. She just had to play her cards right tonight. Plenty women said that good pussy could make a nigga fall in love, and that was exactly what she was banking on. There was only one problem... She hadn't the slightest idea as to how to do that.

"So y'all gon' do that nasty dance, or you just dick-teasing his ass for show?" Kevia asked with one brow lifted and a slick ass smirk on her lips.

"That nigga got a fuckin' pole in his pants, Kee." Star dropped her voice so low that only Kevia could hear and gave her a knowing look that made her crack up laughing.

"You sure you know what to do with it? I know damn well that Travis wasn't workin' with anything close to what Polo got," Kevia replied, and Star couldn't hide the trepidation from her face.

Seeing it made Kevia have to bite down on the smile teasing the edge of her lips. She'd long suspected that Star had been lying about what all went down between her and Travis but hadn't yet called her bluff.

"I think I'm good. You know I ain't no virgin," Star lied, flipping her hair as she rolled her eyes. Her bottom lip twitched a little, a telling sign that she was lying.

"Yeah, that's what your mouth says," Kevia baited her. "But you never told me details about that shit. Did it hurt?"

Caught off guard, Star's thoughts merged, and for once in her life, she was at a loss for some sassy shit to say. Narrowing her eyes, she looked up as if waiting for the answer to fall from the sky.

"Um, it was—"

"Bitch! You a damn lie. You ain't do shit with Travis, did you? Tell the truth!"

Dropping her head, Star decided to just go ahead and come clean. It was better to admit to Kevia that she'd lied and to get advice on how to handle someone like Polo than to hold on to her story and look like a damn fool later on that night.

"Nah, I didn't. I just let him feel on my ass a little, and we kissed. That was it."

"I knew it!" Kevia exclaimed, punching her fist into her other hand. "You ain't gotta lie to kick it, bitch!"

Annoyed, Star rolled her eyes and sat back in her chair. "You ain't gotta rub the shit in. And anyways, after tonight, I'm not gonna be a virgin anymore for real, so it don't matter."

"So my girl gon' let Polo break her in," Kevia said, nodding her head slowly in admiration. "I guess I'm proud of you or whatever." She dramatically rolled her eyes. "You tryin' to be on your grown woman shit."

Picking up on the anxiety all over Star's face, Kevia let out a deep breath and decided that it was time to be a friend. She took a big gulp of her drink and then began to speak.

"A'ight. Before you go in there and embarrass us both by not knowin' a damn thing, let me tell you a few things."

CHAPTER 10

THE DJ DECIDED TO SET THE NIGHT OFF RIGHT AND CHOSE TO PLAY a slow song to give the hopeful niggas praying to get some ass, a head start.

Polo wasn't a part of that group. Yes, he planned on getting some ass, but the last thing he needed was a head start. Even if Star hadn't been more than willing to give him exactly what he was looking for, he'd never been the type to have to rely on something else to help him charm the panties off of any female.

Since the day he was born, he'd gotten accustomed to the fact that there was just something about him that women loved. It didn't matter that he had so many ugly traits. It didn't even matter that he wasn't the finest nigga in his crew... He was always the one the hoes flocked to. Like a moth to a flame, they couldn't resist his swag. He had the air of a champion and the mind of a businessman. Not even the harsh conditions of the ghetto could affect that.

However, the devastation, poverty, violence, and hopelessness around him nearly birthed his entire personality. For someone who made his outside so easy for women to love, his inside couldn't be more of a contrast. He was made from the same thing that demons were made of.

If he had been brought up in another world, belonged to another family... one who believed in taking their son to a therapist once they'd noted his lack of compassion and empathy for others, he'd probably be diagnosed as a sociopath. He had little regard to life, didn't believe on giving second chances, and would cut off key members of his life without a care in the world. He wasn't a wolf in sheep's clothing, because it wasn't his style to ever be considered anything close to a sheep; he was a lion with a dark penchant for violence. He never aspired to be friendly or to blend in with the masses. Polo built his own path, and his mentality was fuck anyone or anything that didn't go along with that.

This was the reason that at only the young age of twenty-five, Polo was already sitting at the head of one of the largest criminal organizations in the United States. Men old enough to be his father, or even grandfather, bowed to his command when they saw him coming, and although he attributed a lot of the respect he'd earned to his own doings, the truth of it was that if it wasn't for Kato, his chief enforcer and best friend, he probably wouldn't have been able to obtain even half of the shit he already did.

Like Polo, Kato didn't have a conscience either and boasted that about as much as he did his 'give no fucks' attitude, but his reckless attitude made him seem even more vicious than Polo. While his friend had a natural charm that initially hid his callousness, Kato wasn't interested in making people like him, and he made no effort to hide that fact. He was mannish, aggressive, and unapologetically so; in actuality, it seemed like he enjoyed inflicting pain on others. He got high off it the same way that some did when it came to drugs. Although Polo appreciated him, he didn't quite understand how necessary it was to his reign to have Kato around, but now that he was in a coma, Polo realized how much he needed his primary enforcer on his team.

Since word got out that his most feared soldier was no longer roaming the Chicago streets, niggas had started getting too relaxed. Polo commanded a tight ship, but it was Kato who actually made sure that things ran smoothly. With him gone, too much shit was popping up that Polo had to handle on his own, and the increased pressure had him on edge. Not only did he need Kato to make a full recovery so that he could really know what had happened that night with Mink, but he also needed him back beating the streets.

Many times, when Polo was looking at Star that night as she danced without a care, giggled with Kevia about whatever girly shit they had on their minds, and stared love-drunkenly into his eyes, he found himself wondering whether she could be trusted. He couldn't shake it no matter how hard he tried. He just had a nagging feeling that shit hadn't gone down quite the way she'd sworn they had. Still, he tried his hardest to push those feelings away because there wasn't a thing. he could do about it. Unless Kato came to, he wouldn't know the truth, but the fact was that time wasn't on his side. The moment to make a move on Star was now, and he didn't want to wait any longer.

"Damn, ma. Yo' body soft as fuck," Polo whispered into Star's ear, making her shiver.

After his brief conversation with Sloan, he began to feel the need to have her by his side and summoned her over. With a smile, she gave in without resistance, her eager eyes showing her willingness to obey his every word.

Being so close to him had her feeling things that she'd only imagined in those times she dreamed about him. But this was real life, even though it still felt like a dream.

He smells so damn good!

Star had no idea what the name of Polo's cologne was, but she knew it was the strongest type of elixir, casting a spell that made her like putty in his hands. She was just a young girl in love and had no idea that she was playing with fire. By the time she would be able to see him through eyes unclouded by her desire, it would be too late because she would already be in too deep.

"You tryin' to go home with me tonight?"

Star nearly flinched at the question. Although she'd wanted him to say those words all night long, she wasn't ready for them when they came. Her words caught in her throat, and her breathing stalled; she felt her body began to tense.

Looking down at her, Polo began to chuckle.

"You scared now? What was all that big shit you was talkin' back in the whip?" he asked her with a teasing smile that she couldn't help but respond to.

Rolling her eyes, she gave him a playful nudge and then cocked her head to the side with her reply.

"I wasn't talkin' big shit. I was tellin' you the truth."

"Prove it then," Polo replied, still smiling. He ran his tongue slowly over his teeth as he waited for her to respond. Not in an intentionally sexual way, but Star felt her pussy throb nonetheless. He was effortlessly fine in ways that even he hadn't picked up on. Or maybe he had. His simplest actions had her caught up beyond saving.

But Star played it coy and stepped back, crossing her arms in front of her chest. She placed her weight on one hip, giving him a good look at her curvy frame, and he did just as she'd intended, licking his lips as his eyes slid from her head down to her toes.

"I can do that right now," she challenged him, her tone just loud enough over the loud music so that only his ears could hear. "In fact, Kevia's cousin got me a room waiting, so I can show you just what I'm workin' with."

In her playful, childish mind, Star was more excited about the tease than the deed. She was talking like a vet when she hadn't even seen a dick in real life. Well, a boy had pulled one out on her in elementary school, but even a virgin knew that if the dick wasn't over six inches, it didn't count. From her estimations, Polo had more than his share to work with, and he wasn't the only one she was trying to convince that she was ready. She was trying to convince herself too.

"You bold as fuck." Polo said it like a compliment, and that's exactly how she took it. "Let's get up out of here. I wanna see what you 'bout."

Star's stomach flip-flopped, but Polo was already grabbing her hand and walking toward the door. It was time to put up or shut up, and she wasn't quite sure which one she wanted to do. Planting her heels firmly into the gym floor, she stopped walking so suddenly that it jerked him backward. He recovered smoothly and then turned, casting his sharp eyes right into Star's.

"I-I need to get my clutch," she stuttered, pulling her hand from his so that she could tug nervously at a stray lock of hair. "I'll be back."

Before he could object, she walked back to the table where she'd left her things, purposely passing right by Kevia, who was slow-grinding against Sloan on the dancefloor.

"Come with me!" she hissed through her teeth in Kevia's direction while wrinkling her brow slightly to let her know that it was urgent.

Kevia didn't hesitate to follow behind her, leaving Sloan behind to recover from the sexual trance her wide ass had been placing him in. Clearing his throat, he ran his hand over his mouth and then covertly nudged down the erection that Kevia was responsible for. Once that was taken care of, he watched the girls as they chattered amongst each other in between tossing glances at something near the front. He followed their eyes and inwardly groaned when he saw Polo standing there. It didn't take long to see the look in his eyes and pick up on exactly what was about to go down that night.

Clicking his teeth, Sloan shook his head, knowing that Star was as good as gone. Once Polo had his eyes on her, it was a wrap. Niggas like him got their lifeline from the women they were with—draining them of their confidence, strength, and vitality until there was nothing but an empty shell left. Only then would he allow her to leave; once she was worthless to him. He'd done the same thing to Tonya, who had grown up so innocent, sheltered, and bright, until she met Polo.

It was crazy how being with the wrong nigga could take everything from a woman when being with the wrong bitch never seemed to take all that much from a man, beyond his peace of mind. Women gave their all in love—they were programmed to sacrifice for the sake of the ones they cared for. It was the way that God made it, and that was why no one could love harder than a woman. She loved with her whole heart, and for this reason, for so many women, love was their downfall.

Giving a man your *whole* heart—that's a powerful thing because if he fucks that up, you've got nothing left but emptiness, and that was the type of shit that made you bitter. Messing with Polo was about to make Star just another bitter bitch, and yeah, Sloan was disappointed by that, but it was really none of his business. Of all things murdered in the hood, hopes and dreams were the most prevalent victims.

"That bitch about to go get *turned out!*" Kevia shrieked as she danced her way back toward Sloan. He crooked his brow as he looked at her, a sly smile rising up on his face.

"What's that lil' jig you just did? Don't tell me chicks got a special dance for when they home girl about to get some." Sloan laughed. "What they do when I put the dick on you?"

"I don't let females all in my business!" Kevia snapped with a half-lie.

True, she didn't tell her homegirls about anything dealing with Sloan unless it was Star. Of all the girls Kevia hung with, Star was the only one she could trust around her man. Star was a true friend, and that was why their connection was so pure. Kevia wouldn't ever betray Star for a man and vice versa. They weren't competitive in that way.

"I hope she knows what she's getting into," Sloan said, delivering his final warning. "That nigga Polo ain't playin' with this gang shit. He's true with it. Tonya used to get her ass whooped like a grown man for fuckin' with dude."

Caught off guard by his comment, Kevia's neck snapped back. She sucked her teeth and cut her eyes at him before speaking out the side of her mouth.

"Boy, please! You know Star ain't the type to let no man, nigga, or bitch put their hands on her. She been fighting since the day I met her."

Silent, Sloan simply nodded his head. Kevia had to grow up faster than most girls her age being that she pretty much raised her sisters and brothers, but she still was so naïve about life. She didn't understand how life could humble you—push you into doing shit you never thought you'd do. The part of her that was still hopeful and positive was preserved, even though she lived in such a hopeless place. That was what drew him to her in the beginning. But Sloan knew better than to look at things the way she did.

"You might be right," he said, pretending to contemplate her words for a short while.

In the next second, he'd pushed thoughts about Star and Polo from his mind, focusing instead on the bombshell before his eyes.

Unlike Star, Kevia wasn't thick, but she had just enough ass for him to work with. Her skin was shiny and dark as coal, her hair was coarse with a subtle wave, and she glued her baby hairs down with black gel, forming soft ringlets that fit her unique hairstyles. She was her own person, as loyal as they came, and he loved that about her. No matter what he took her through—and it was a lot—she always stuck around, and that was why he knew he could never let her go. She would bear his seed and take his last name... once he was ready to settle down.

"Can you stay with me tonight?" Kevia asked with her head cocked to the side, trying her luck.

When Sloan took a step back and sighed, her heart dropped. He didn't have to say a word. She already knew what was coming next.

"You know I can't do that."

"Why not?" She pouted, poking out her bottom lip. "This is prom night. You can't figure something out to tell her?"

Sloan pressed his lips firmly together, a sign that he wasn't planning to respond. With a huff, Kevia gave up the fight with little resistance. If she pouted too much, it would only push Sloan away. The reason he said he loved her so much was because she made it so easy. She knew all his truths and never judged him for it. She was his peace, and she had to let it stay that way or risk losing him for good... the little piece of himself he gave to her anyways.

"How long before you gotta go?" she asked with a pitiful whine.

She hated the way her voice sounded. How sad was it to be the only chick in the room who had a man refusing to spend the night with her? Niggas were in here wishing on their lucky stars that they could get even one girl to give him some personal attention, and here she was, getting turned down by the one who belonged to her.

Nah, this nigga ain't *mine, and that's the fuckin' problem*, she thought to herself.

"I'll stay until 'round three, then I gotta head out, or my baby moms will start trippin'. That work for you?" Sloan waged. Then seeing the sour look on her face, he tried to appease her with a lopsided grin, showing off dimples that she thought were just so cute. "We can do whatever you want until then."

Something about the way he said it forced her to forget all about being mad. The boyish, teasing look in his eyes, the way his waves swirled around his head in perfect circles that she loved to trace with her fingers while he lay beside her in the bed, the thick, long snake he was holding in his pants... all of those things played a part in her pushing away her disappointment so that she could enjoy the moment. He didn't even have to try hard; she was eager to forgive him because her heart already wanted to.

Sloan held all the power over her, and he knew it, even if he tried not to abuse it. Kevia had no idea that she was pushing herself into a position that she'd more than likely never escape from. Regardless to what he said about how he felt about her, she was third in his life, and he was comfortable with that because she allowed it to be that way.

"Okaaayyy," Kevia sang out, smiling hard. She hadn't won the battle or the war, but she felt lucky for any opportunity she got to be with Sloan. "But let's stop wasting time and get the hell out of here."

Grabbing his hand, she led Sloan out of the gym, pushing through the crowd as butterflies fluttered around in the pit of her stomach. In all the time that she'd been messing with him, he still had the power to make her excited and anxious to be in his arms. Maybe it was because she knew she was working with borrowed time and that she had to cherish every moment. Maybe it was because she still couldn't believe that a man like him would actually be interested in someone like her— the Black girl with skin as dark as the pavement who was used to people using her looks against her.

More times than she could count, she'd been made fun of for her complexion. Though she'd never admit it, even *she* thought of it as a disability sometimes—like something she had to overcome by over-compensating in other ways, usually sexually. Deep down, that was why she never gave Sloan much of a problem when he gave her less than she deserved... and why she let him fuck on the first night. She didn't have light skin, long hair, or a fat ass like the other girls, so she felt it was only right to do other things to make herself more desirable. Made perfect sense, right? The very things about her that she should have cherished, she saw as a vice.

Biting down on his bottom lip, Sloan tugged her back by her hand, scooping her body into his arms. Carrying her like she was his bride rather than his poorly-hidden side chick, Sloan kissed her lips and cradled her to his chest the entire way to the car.

"I love you," he whispered into her ear, and she giggled, feeling her whole body tingle with a warm feeling.

"I love you more," she told him, and it was the truth. She did love Sloan—much more than he loved her. Very soon, she would realize how much of a problem that was.

CHAPTER 11

Bunching her lips into her mouth, Star took a deep breath and pressed her hands flat against her thighs to stop herself from wringing them nervously in front her. Excited energy fluttered through her body and she couldn't squash the fact that she was still so nervous about what was supposed to happen next.

Relax, she told herself, forcing her head back against Polo's dark chocolate leather headrest. His whip was so nice that, once again, she found herself thinking of what it would be like to be his lady. Being with him was a high in itself but the thought of having access to all the finer things in life took her over the moon.

Then the phone rang once more through the speakers of the car, and she noticed Polo cast a long glance at her before he answered it.

It was the same deep baritone sounding voice from the last phone call that she had overheard.

"Aye, man. I'm kinda on a mission. I got a birthday gift to deliver," Polo said with a chuckle and glanced at Star's sensuous thighs with a smirk. Her cheeks went warm and she turned slightly to look out the window.

"Yo, I got bad news... We can't move on that shit tonight. The nigga said he had some shit to do and couldn't meet up."

Star snuck a glance at Polo and caught his reaction as his mood changed from playful into clipped rage. His jaw clenched tight, and the heat coming from him was so tangible that she could almost see steam surrounding the space around him.

"He might be on to her," the voice continued. "He knows she's a Gangstress, one of the loyal ones, so she probably gave in too easy. A chick who isn't as known for always being around would be better to use. Got any ideas?"

With that said, Polo rolled his eyes over to Star and gave her a hard look. She kept her attention pointed forward, pretending not to feel the heat of his stare on her. Her breath stalled in her lungs as she waited for whatever it was he'd say next. If he offered her up to his enemy as prey, she'd have to go along with it for fear of the punishment that would follow going against his orders, but she would be heart-broken all the same.

"Nah, not at the moment," Polo said finally, before sighing and turning away from her. It was only then that Star was able to relax. "I'll shoot you some names later, a'ight."

Before the man could respond, Polo simply hung up the phone.

They drove in silence, Star's nerves on edge as he wove in and out of lanes. The air between them was thick—Polo was submerged in his own thoughts, and she was deep in her own. Finally, he made a sudden turn that made her peer out the window, noticing that they were nowhere near the motel that she had given him the directions to.

"Um... where are we goin'?" she dared to ask, trying to calm her tone although she could hear the tremble in her own voice. "The room I got for us is the other way. You should've made a left back—"

"I know where I'm going," Polo interjected, not even glancing in her direction. "Just chill out. You actin' like a nigga tryin' to kidnap your ass or somethin'."

Exhaling heavily, Star forced herself to sink into the seat and kept her mouth closed. Although she had dreamt of being alone with him so many times, her body was in an uproar—as if it was sending signals to her that she was about to make a mistake. She was raw with anxiety, so much so that she could barely sit still. Chewing on the side of her mouth, she tapped her stiletto heels rhythmically against the car floor and tried to calm her nerves.

Sensing that something was off with her, Polo cut his eyes in Star's direction, and one glance told him everything that he needed to know. She was trippin' for real.

This why I don't like fuckin' with these young chicks who used to talkin' shit, he told himself, suspicious that Star's statements about her promiscuous life were a lie. If it were, that would be a good thing, but he would have liked to know that in advance so he could have slipped her a little something to take the edge off. Nothing got a virgin in the mood better than poppin' a Molly or takin' a little sip of syrup.

"Shit," he said, glancing down in his cup holders.

He usually kept a pill or two in the car just for times like this. Raising the dash, he pushed his hand inside and felt around as Star stared at him with wide eyes. Taking another peek at her, he almost started to laugh. The deer-caught-in-headlights expression on her face made it easy to see that she had finally came to the realization that she was fuckin' with a real nigga, and that meant anything goes. Every movement he made, she watched it carefully as if she was prepared to jump right out of the moving car at any minute.

"Aye, take this."

Before she got a chance to ask what it was, he popped something in his mouth and then pushed a white pill against her lips. She frowned, but the pressure of his eyes on hers, waiting for her to take it in, was too great. Star was young, and even though she was strong-minded and smart, she was still easily manipulated by a man. With no father in her life and a mama who wasn't 'bout shit, she had no one to warn her against things that came as common sense to other girls who had someone looking out for their virtues.

"What is it?" she asked, screwing up her face. The pill had a sour taste. Reaching down, Polo grabbed a bottle of water, took a swig, and then handed it to her.

"It's something that will make you feel good," he replied, and she nodded, taking the water from his hand.

"You took one too?" she asked, and he nodded his head without saying a word.

It was a lie. The only thing he'd placed in his mouth was a Tic Tac. Polo didn't do any drugs, not even weed, and he didn't drink. The paranoia that came with his lifestyle was like a curse—he was already reminded that there were hundreds of niggas on the streets who wanted him dead. Even when he wanted to forget that fact long enough to relax, he couldn't, because he was reminded of it even in his dreams.

At only thirteen-years-old, he'd seen his father gunned down right in front of their home by a nigga Polo had grown up calling his uncle. For that reason, he didn't trust any man on God's green Earth. Kato was the only exception because of how long he'd known him, but he kept a close eye on him too.

The drug almost took an immediate effect on Star. Before she knew it, not only was the anxiety gone, but she even found herself rapping along to the song on the radio, waving her hands in the air as she cut up in her seat with her own dance moves. Smirking, Polo eyed her as she grinded her wide hips against his seat, simulating riding a dick. She was thick and juicy... He didn't eat pussy, but one look at her thick ass thighs had him really considering making a few changes.

"Where are we?" Star inquired, frowning as they pulled up to a hotel entrance much ritzier than the one she had secured for them. There was valet standing out front and everything! Never in life had she even been near something so luxurious. It was something straight out of a movie.

"This is where our room is," he replied. He pulled the car up and waited for the valet to walk up to his door.

"So you don't want to stay in the other room?"

"I don't believe in letting a woman treat me. Save your money... I got this," he told her, and she smiled from ear-to-ear in response.

The valet approached Polo's side of the car and waited while he took his time before rolling down the window. He seemed to operate on his own timing when it came to all things.

"Aye, I'll pay for valet, but I'm gonna park it myself, a'ight?"

The man wrinkled his brow but then nodded his head. He didn't understand the request, but he wasn't about to argue about being paid for doing less work. Pointing ahead of them, he gave Polo instructions on where to park his car and then stepped back to allow them to drive by. Polo's entourage of henchmen followed close behind.

"Why you didn't just let them do it?" Star asked, curious as well about Polo's request.

But really, she had been itching to get the valet experience just like she'd seen before on TV. She was anticipating the moment the attendant would walk to her side, open her door, and help her out while calling her 'madame'. She would have giggled and tossed him a cute smile the same way she'd seen Gabrielle Union do in a movie once.

"I don't let nobody drive my shit," Polo replied, and she nearly rolled her eyes. He seemed to have so many rules about what he did and didn't do. Star didn't know it, but this wasn't even half of it. Polo had rules for *everything*, but she would find out about all that soon enough.

Besides, even if she missed the valet experience, it was nothing in comparison to this hotel he'd brought her to. To stay in a place that looked like it didn't have a single roach or rat anywhere in a mile radius around it, was an incredible thought. She could actually jump into the bed without checking under covers for critters and sleep without the covers pulled up over her head to keep bugs from crawling in her mouth at night. These were little things that other people took for granted, but to Star, that was just her life.

"I can't believe you brought me here." She gushed as they got out of the car.

"Get used to this shit," Polo told her like it was nothing. "I only get and give the best." He shot her a look that set her sex on fire.

The tingling that was in her belly moved to the space between her thighs. The pill may have had something to do with it, but Star didn't think so. She attributed all of her good feelings to the man by her side. Everything Polo said and did was so sweet, so charming, and so worthy of her love. Being a girl who had never known a man to drop cash on her for anything without even giving it a second thought, Star was shocked by his generosity. To go the extra mile to spend all this money when he barely knew her... it was unheard of.

I can't wait to tell Kevia about this shit!

She checked her clutch to make sure that she had her cell phone with her. She was going to take as many pics as her phone could hold as soon as she got the chance. If she weren't so afraid of being looked at as someone who wasn't used to this kind of treatment, she would have already been all on SnapChat and Instagram live, but Polo's nonchalant attitude made her calm down. She didn't want to embarrass him, especially not when he'd done something so nice. It was already bad enough that they were attracting the attention of a few people standing around wondering why they were being followed by a team of goons.

Star was giving Polo credit for something that she shouldn't have. His words led her to believe that coming to this hotel was about her, but the truth was that he was really looking out for himself. Had he been a less cautious man, she would have been sliding her ass right against the hard, crusty sheets at the Motel 8 that Kevia's cousin had gotten for them.

Although Star may have forgotten it, Polo clearly remembered Tonya saying that Kevia mentioned her cousin being a Blood right before she shot her in the leg. Staying in any place arranged by the member of a rival gang was probably the dumbest way to get caught slipping, and he was too smart for that. A legendary street champ, Polo didn't make a name for himself by being a dumb ass nigga, and the fact that he wanted to fuck Star more than anything right then wasn't enough to make him into one. That was also the reason why only a couple trustworthy people knew where he laid his head, and he always slept alone. Even Tonya had never slept in the same bed as him. He didn't trust a woman enough to be that vulnerable around her. Too many times he'd seen a nigga fall at the hands of a woman he thought loved him.

The entrance of the hotel was even more majestic than the outside. In the middle of the lobby hung a chandelier that was expensive enough to buy every house on Star's block... but even it wasn't the costliest piece in the room. Everything screamed money and it made Star feel slightly self-conscious. If all this screamed money, did everything about her scream broke?

Standing just a few feet behind Polo, she watched as he checked them in. He was so comfortable around white people, which was crazy to her because she was *never* at ease around them. Their eyes always looked at her in a judging way, like she was beneath them or didn't fit in their world. Even when it came to her teachers, no matter what their mouths said, their eyes told it all. They didn't expect much from her when they first met her. They always just figured she was just another hood bunny with no education that they'd have to put up with, until she proved them wrong.

"Show time," Polo told her once he was done, and she walked over to him, feeling giddy.

He signaled to his men something only they could decipher, and the largest one of the crew walked to the front desk as well. Star had no idea what he was up to, but she didn't care. She was just happy knowing that they weren't following them to the elevator. Finally, they would really be alone outside of the car.

THE DRUG WAS REALLY TAKING effect.

Star felt so high and alive, like she was experiencing life for the very first time. Standing beside Polo, she got the urge to touch him, and this time, she felt courageous enough to make the first move. Suppressing a slick smile, she reached out and pushed the tips of her fingers lightly against the palm of his hands.

Polo lifted one brow and glanced at her. The childish excitement in her eyes made him chuckle. He grabbed her hand, lacing her fingers through his and then pressed the 'P' button to start the elevator. Star frowned at the illuminated button, wondering what it stood for.

"How much did this room cost you?" Star asked him as they rode up to the top floor. Her ears popped, and she flinched, feeling a little lightheaded.

While sending a text, Polo shrugged and let the answer slip from his lips like it was nothing.

"About a grand."

Star nearly lost her mind. Her eyes bugged out of her skull like they were about to pop out and roll across the floor in front of them. She could barely believe her ears.

Oh my God!

A grand for one night! It took her months of doing hair and

makeup to even come close to that amount, and here he was, tossing the cash over like it was five bucks. He didn't have a care in the world —couldn't have one—at least not any that money couldn't solve. How freeing it had to be to have that type of money at your disposal. She didn't understand that Polo was in as much of a prison to the Chicago street life as she was, even if his prison was in the suburbs and surrounded by all kinds of luxury that she'd never be able to afford.

The doors to the elevator opened right into the room. Marveling, Star stepped off the elevator behind Polo, realizing that they had the entire floor to themselves.

P stands for penthouse! she thought, as it finally soaked in.

Although she tried to hide it, her amazement was obvious, but not even in her wildest dreams had she ever considered that this could be part of her life—walking her department store heels across heated tile floors made for kings and queens. He was giving her a glimpse of the good life.

"Why don't you go ahead and get cleaned up," Polo told her like a statement rather than a question as he texted from his phone with a deep frown on his face. "Should be a robe or some shit for you to put on once you're done. I'll be on the balcony handling business."

He didn't have to say it twice. As soon as he closed the glass doors to the balcony, she zipped around the room like the Roadrunner, checking out everything as fast as she could. With her cell phone high in the air, she took a few kissy-face selfies for Instagram and then sent a couple to Kevia. She was going to be *so jealous* when she saw them. Sloan dished out a lot of cash, but he'd never done anything close to this!

The bathroom was so regal; she felt childish for even referring to it as a bathroom because it was so much more. Rich people probably called it a 'lavatory' or some shit. The toilet was so clean and pristine, she figured that this was what white people would call a 'commode'. There was another toilet right next to the normal looking one, and it had handles on it like a faucet.

"Damn," she whispered while recording it all on SnapChat. "Rich people don't even shit regular! Look at this!"

Star had never before seen a Jacuzzi tub, and it took her a minute to figure out how to turn on the jets, but as soon as she got it going, she peeled off her dress and jumped right in. Next to the tub was a small bottle of bubble bath, and she emptied the entire thing into it, squealing with excitement when the jets made the bubbles sprout right up. She dipped her toes in the water, testing the heat before dropping her body in. With her hair tied up high on the top of her head, she laid all the way back and enjoyed the feel of the soapy water against her skin. The moment was perfect—this was the way every girl should have ended her prom night, but many would not. Star was just happy to be one of the lucky ones.

She spread her legs open and allowed the jets to shoot water between her thighs, and a jolt of sexual energy shot through her. Her lips parted and let out a happy sigh. The jets felt good, but it had to be nothing in comparison to what Polo was about to put on her. All of her anxiety about that moment was gone. If anything let her know that he was the one, this right here sure did. Hell, after dropping a whole stack on the room alone, he deserved the pussy! All them other bitches at prom were giving up the panties to niggas who couldn't even afford half of this shit, but she had saved her cookie for a boss.

"You look relaxed as fuck. Forgot all about me, huh?"

Star opened her eyes and was pleased to see Polo hovering over her, looking down as she soaked in the tub. Feeling playful, she smirked and then lifted her knees in the air slowly before spreading them from east to west. The bubbles were placed just right to cover up her treasure box, but he knew exactly what she was suggesting. His lips curved into a smile, and he took off his shirt, exposing his rock-hard abs, keeping his thick gold chain dangling around his neck. Although he'd posted plenty of pictures on his Instagram with his shirt off, this was the first time that Star got a chance to see his tattoos up close.

They covered his entire upper body, making it look like he still had on a shirt although he wasn't wearing one. He turned around to place his shirt behind him and she eyed the tattooed six-pointed star with pitchforks sitting right between his shoulder blades on his back; the Gangster Disciples' signature tattoo. Most Disciples didn't get it tatted for fear of being caught up by the police and automatically deemed guilty by association. It was obvious that Polo didn't gave no fucks about that.

Reaching in the water, he wrapped his arms around both sides of Star's body and pulled her right out of the water, soaking wet.

"What are you doing!" she shrieked, laughing. He didn't answer. With her in his arms, he walked right over to the bed and dumped her on top of the premium white sheets. Star nearly jumped straight out of the bed.

"You're going to mess the sheets up! I'm so wet!"

"That's exactly how I want you," Polo replied, smiling suggestively.

She giggled and fell back on to the bed, shrugging like 'what the hell'. This was his money, and if he didn't care, neither did she. Plus, this wasn't the only bed in the room; they could just sleep on another one later.

Leaning back on his legs, Polo unzipped his jeans and let them drop to his ankles before pulling his thick pole out of the opening of his Gucci boxers. Star's eyes grew wide as she looked at it, feeling a mixture of emotions somewhere between lust and love. He had a beautiful dick—long and fat with a smooth milk chocolate complexion. Licking her lips, it was like her body already knew what she was supposed to do with it. Her mind erupted with all kinds of salacious thoughts.

"What you gon' do with this?" Polo grinned, his gold teeth sparkling in the dim light.

Star didn't need any more of an invitation. She was ready to do exactly as Kevia had instructed her.

"You gotta take that shit all the way down your throat, like this," Kevia had instructed her in the bathroom during prom. *"And use your tongue on the head while you do it. Niggas can't resist that shit. Make sure your mouth is really wet... use a lot of slob. If they got mouthwash in the motel, swallow some down and it'll trick up your gag reflex. It sounds kinda weird, but niggas love it. Trust me."*

Grabbing on to the base of Polo's dick in the way that she'd been instructed to, she sucked him in and went too fast, trying to immediately force him right down her throat. She'd barely gotten a good two inches in before gagging. Tears stung her eyes, and she coughed. Maybe she actually did need the mouthwash.

"Suck that dick, baby," Polo told her, guiding her head back over to where he wanted it.

He pushed his hips forward slightly so that the head of his penis was pressed right against her lips, awaiting entry. Squashing the tears, she cleared her throat and then opened her mouth once more, allowing him to guide her movements with his hand at the back of her head. She let her mouth go limp; she couldn't keep up with his speed. To him, she looked like a dead fish, her mouth wide open with her tongue lapping around pitifully inside.

"Hold them lips tight, ma. Use your tongue... Damn, you ain't never sucked a dick?"

Taking a step back, he pulled himself from her lips and looked down at her with narrowed eyes. Star thought about lying but then changed her mind and shook her head 'no'. She felt defeated by her ignorance. He had done all of this, and she couldn't even perform in a way that seemed so simple.

"Word? What niggas you been fuckin' that ain't want no head?" he pressed, totally confused. The expression that passed through Star's eyes answered his question. Shocked, he teetered only for a second before laughing out loud.

"Damn, so you been full of shit this whole time, huh? You a virgin, huh?"

Star dropped her head low and nodded, feeling more than a little embarrassed even though the euphoric feeling from the drug still had some effect, though mild, now that her lies had been exposed. Reaching down, Polo lifted her head by placing two fingers under her chin.

"Aye, that's a good thing," he told her and then continued on when he saw the confusion in her eyes. "I couldn't fuck with you on no serious level if you had already been spoiled. Since you're pure, I can really make you mine."

Spoiled?

Star was still confused by his statement, but she pushed that away to focus on the last part of what he said. *I can really make you mine.* Did that mean that after tonight, she'd officially be his?

"Get up and get on your knees," he said, and she obeyed. He switched sides with her, sitting on the bed.

"I'm going to teach you how to suck my dick. Since I'm the only nigga you'll ever fuck with from now on, I'm the only one you need to worry about pleasin', so I'll make sure you know how to do the shit the way I like."

So excited about the prospect of being his only one, Star neglected to ask about her own pleasure. What about her being *his* only one? And would he learn what it took to please her? The lesson that sex was only for men and it was only about his pleasure was so deeply ingrained in her head that it didn't even occur to her that he wasn't the least bit concerned about making her satisfied.

"Here it is. Take it in your hands. Don't be scared," he instructed her, and once again, she obeyed without protest. "Now ease your mouth on it, sucking it like a lollipop."

She did just as he said, imagining that his dick was a cherry Tootsie Roll Pop. Polo watched her with his eyes shining. There was something powerful about teaching a woman how to pleasure him, and for someone who was addicted to control, it did wonders to his ego. Placing his hand on the back of her head, he pushed down further toward the back of her throat, watching so intently that he didn't blink as she squinted and tried to take in his length without gagging.

He began to grow to his full length, and Star nearly panicked; her eyes and mouth watered, and she just knew she was going to throw up, but he kept pushing in further, speeding up her motion until she tried to pull back. But he wouldn't let her and only forced her down to take in more. She wasn't good at it, but she would get there. Still, he was turned on because for him, it was all about the power he had over her and not exactly what she was doing to him. Star didn't know it, but this was the beginning of a dangerous cycle where she would squash her own desires in order to please him. She was learning more than one lesson that night.

"Take that shit. Don't run," he coaxed her, lifting his hips to throw his dick deeper.

She retched, but he only went in harder. She had to learn, and he was going to teach her. Closing his eyes, he let her do her thing for a little while, but it was starting to feel like a tease. He needed more. One thing about Tonya, over the years, she had learned exactly how to please him to the max, but it had taken a few hard lessons to get her to that point. If Star was going to live up to that, she was going to have to go through them as well.

Lifting up, he rotated around so that he was standing, and she was sitting against the bed, her head lying on the mattress for support.

"Open up," he told her, and as soon as Star did as he asked, he pushed his dick straight down her throat.

She panicked, but there was nowhere to go. Before she knew it, he was fucking her mouth and throat without compassion, jamming his pole straight down her throat like it was a pussy, pushing past her tonsils. Her eyes stung with tears, and she burped and gagged, screaming out for him to stop, but he didn't. When she lifted her hands to push him, he slapped them away until he got sick of it and simply pinned both of her wrists down on the bed under his hands as he smashed his dick between her jaws.

Star's teeth grazed over his dick, and he grabbed her by the throat, squeezing so hard that her eyes popped.

"Don't fuckin' bite me," he ordered through his teeth, his voice and eyes so cold that they sent shivers down her spine.

"I'm sorry," she gasped, sucking in a few breaths once he released her. "I didn't mean to."

"Just don't let that shit happen again," he replied angrily as he rubbed the head. Looking back at Star, he saw the hurt in her eyes. She was scared, confused, upset, embarrassed... Polo cursed himself, remembering that she was new at this. If he was going to train her, it was better if she was relaxed.

"Aye, my bad about that shit," he somewhat apologized. "I ain't mean to snap like that."

Reaching down, he squeezed her chocolate drop nipples, and a feeling riveted down her spine and rested right in between the lips of her pussy. She looked at him, waiting for him to tell her what to do next.

"I want to teach you how to work this dick, but I gotta pop that cherry first. Lay back on the bed."

"Do-don't we need a condom?" she asked him, feeling nervous all of a sudden. Her eyes danced around the room toward the elevator. She was thinking of taking a run for it—wished she could—but she felt trapped, so she stayed put.

"A condom?" he snapped, frowning. "For what? You a virgin, and I won't nut in you because I don't want kids. Even if I do nut in you, I'll just get you one of them pills or some shit so you don't get pregnant."

Pressing her lips together into a straight line, Star accepted his statement without even thinking of her own safety. Sure, she was a virgin, but he *wasn't*. A lot of women got caught up in the worst of ways for trusting a sick dick, and she was setting herself up to be one of the number.

Getting her cherry popped was about as pleasant as it sounded. Polo didn't take it easy on her, whispering in her ear that it was better not to ease it in but to just get it over with it. He was aggressive and mannish, nothing like what she'd expected. She always thought that when she gave her love to him, it would be a gentle and beautiful experience. This was anything but that.

Nudging his way through her honeypot with all the gentility of an ogre, Polo took her innocence as if it belonged to him, not caring at all to make the experience pleasurable to her. He wasn't patient; he just wanted to get a nut. And even though Star was acting like an unwilling participant, he knew that like all the others before her, she would get over it and fall in love with him anyways.

All women had a special place in their heart for their first because, secretly, most of them wanted that man to be the first and the last one they fucked with. They'd take a lot of bullshit from him that they wouldn't from anyone else. It was this thought that Polo banked on, and that's why it didn't appeal to him to do any more than just steal what she was convincing herself that she was freely handing over.

"Now we can really get going," Polo said, seeming proud of himself once he pulled his dick from her and saw blood smeared all over the head.

"Okay," Star said, forcing a smile on her face.

Her insides were burning, and she felt so sore, but... maybe this was how it was supposed to be. This wasn't like it seemed to be on TV, but the more she thought about it, nothing was. One of her favorite shows to watch was old reruns of *Sex in the City*, and she'd spent plenty of times watching Sarah Jessica Parker and her friends jump from bed to bed with sexy man after man, having the most amazing sexual experiences before they pulled on their three-hundred-dollar Manolos and trotted off to their beautiful Manhattan apartments. She had spent so many nights imagining that this could be her life, but she was wrong. The sex was painful, she lived in the Chicago slums instead of a high-rise, and instead of Manolos, she wore thirty-dollar heels on her feet. Maybe this was just how life really was for people like her.

"Turn around and get on your knees. Push your ass up in the air," Polo commanded her, and once again like a loyal subject, she did just that.

With a hard slap on her backside, he inserted his throbbing pole right into her folds, making her scream out in pain. She squeezed the creamy sheets on the bed with her long acrylic nails so hard that one of them broke in two.

"I'll take it slow," he whispered right before he got started, giving her a little sense of hope.

But it was a lie.

Polo did *not* take it slow. In many rap songs, Star had heard a man bragging about how he was about to 'murder that pussy', but she'd always taken it as a figure of speech. No, it was nothing but the fuckin' truth, because that's exactly what it felt like Polo did. What he was doing felt like pure pussy homicide. His nails tore at her skin as he grabbed her ass, slamming it back against his lap. He snatched at her waist, forcing her to keep her hips lifted, and pushed down at her back, increasing her arch. She yelled out, screaming in pain, but he didn't stop.

"Noooo!" she whimpered near tears, but he ignored her and continued the assault.

This was nothing short of rape, but Star still did her best to make the experience pleasurable for him. He had spent so much money on her, given her such a great time that night. He had blessed her with his presence, and this was her way of thanking him. Didn't he deserve to have a good time?

Tears streamed down her cheeks, and she bit down on her bottom lip to stay quiet as he pummeled her insides. His movements were hard, jagged, and savage like an animal. Nothing like the soft gentle caresses she had been prepared for.

With a loud guttural grunt, he groaned so loudly that the sound rang in her ears and then he pulled himself from her. She allowed her face to drop onto the sheets, and her body went limp onto the bed as he sprinkled her body with his seed, spraying what felt like buckets of sticky liquid all over her.

"You got some good pussy," he said, sucking his teeth lightly as she lay in the bed, recovering. "Damn, I think I might fall in love with that shit."

Even in the midst of her misery, Star's heart jumped at the mention of love. Rolling over, she pressed her thighs together and pulled up the wet sheets to hide her body. For some reason, there was a sense of shame in her heart now that wasn't present before. She felt the need to hide from him.

"You know you're mine now, right?" he asked, smiling.

Star couldn't resist the boyish grin on his face and found herself smiling back at him. Her pussy still ached as if shards of glass had been dragged across her clit, but her little young heart was so quick to forgive the man that she'd wanted for so long. In her mind, she felt like he'd given her a gift by letting her have his body when, in actuality, the only one doing the giving that night was her.

"You mean that?" she asked.

Polo licked his lips and nodded before pulling on his jeans and sitting beside her on the bed. The entire time they'd had sex, he hadn't even completely taken off his clothes. He had fucked her with his pants around his ankles, shoes and boxers still on. This was a moment she would remember for the rest of her life, and he hadn't even bothered to fully disrobe, fucking her in haste like she was a little thot he'd picked up in the club for the night.

Star was too caught up in him to even care. She was pressed to make this moment mean something for herself, even if it was nothing to him.

"I'm your first... Do you know what that means?" he posed, and she thought for a minute before shaking her head. "It means that you belong to me. No other nigga better lay a hand on your body but me. And if any nigga does, he gon' be a dead nigga, and you'll be right beside him. It's me and you until the grave. Got that?"

To Star, those were the sweetest words anyone had ever spoken.

Curling up by his side, Star laid on top of his chest and pressed her ear against his chest, listening to his heart beat.

This is love, she thought as she allowed her mind to dream of how their future would be from here.

She was Polo's girl, officially, just as he'd said. Once the words left his lips, they were made into law. No other man would touch her body, and she would be the down chick by his side for the rest of her life. Once word got out, she knew that she'd have a lot to deal with, but she was ready for the challenge. Those bitches could do what they did best and hate all day until they were blue in the face. She had the man of her dreams by her side, and that was how it would remain.

CHAPTER 12

THE NEXT MORNING CAME, AND POLO WAS NOWHERE TO BE FOUND.

Yawning, Star stretched her arms high above her head and spread her body out. The painful ache between her thighs reminded her of the activities from the night before. Her cheeks tingled with shame when she thought about how different that experience had been in comparison to the way she'd imagined it, but then she remembered Polo's words.

It's me and you until the grave. Got that?

If she was his now... then at least all the pain wasn't for nothing.

Or was it?

The thought circled around in her head as she stood up and walked from the bedroom out into the main part of the penthouse suite, wondering where he was. Every empty room made her heart beat even harder within her chest.

"The hell did he go?" she whispered after opening the bathroom door and seeing that there was no one inside.

A haunting feeling started from her toes and then crept upward until it covered her entire body. Had he left? Discarded her like trash after he'd gotten what he wanted? It wouldn't be the first time a nigga fucked a chick and left her ass hanging, however, Star had never considered that this would happen to her. Especially not after what he'd said... He was a man of his word, right? That had to count for something.

Running over to where she'd placed her clutch, Star reached in and grabbed her cell phone to send him a text.

Where are you?

Biting down on her bottom lip, she waited for his reply, but when none came after a few minutes of sitting there, looking about as dumb as she felt, her eyes began to fill up with tears. This feeling of worthlessness was something new for her. This wasn't the first time that someone had made her feel like she wasn't worth shit, but this time, it was different.

Although Roxy never spoke to her in the way other mothers did, telling their little girls that their virginity was precious and something to protect and only give to a man that they loved and who loved them back, Star did value it in her own way. She'd planned to give it to Polo as a gift, and like a silly immature little girl, she'd assumed that he would see it in that way as well. Obviously, she'd been wrong.

Glancing behind her at the bed, her eyes fell on the bloodstains on the sheets, and she wanted to cry, but something clicked on the inside and gave way to her rage.

If that nigga played me... she thought, smashing one fist into the other, knowing full well that she wasn't going to do a damn thing.

What *could* she do? It happened all the time. A lost in love little girl would give up her goods to a man, thinking it would turn into love only to get a broken heart instead. She wasn't any different from them, and how foolish was it to entertain the idea that she was—or that Polo was any different from any other man? Truthfully, in Star's mind, he just did what niggas do. It didn't matter that she had imagined him to be the exception to the norm. In the end, he was just another nigga.

"Fuck 'em," Star grumbled as she got dressed and snatched up her phone. Stuffing it into her purse, she paused only to cheek her appearance in the bathroom mirror.

The black streaks of mascara and smudged eyeliner was a stinging reminder of everything that had gone on the night before. Sucking her teeth, she furiously turned the faucet on and waited for the water to heat before cleaning her face. It was bad enough that she still felt the agonizing sting of Polo's assault against her between her legs, she refused to *look* like a victim too.

Once her face was clean and her hair was pulled up into a neat ponytail, she marched out the room, making about as much noise as a crew of three, and smashed the button for the lobby on the elevator.

"I can't *wait* until I see that bowlegged, toad-face muthafucka!" she raved, growing angrier by the second.

She was talking big because she knew she couldn't do shit whenever the moment came that she saw Polo again. He was untouchable—a street king with a crew of goons backing his every word. To go toe-to-toe with Polo about anything was like committing suicide. To Star, that was the most embarrassing part of it all. Never in life had she not taken revenge on anyone who had done her wrong, and in the matter of a few months, she felt like both Tonya and Polo were owed a good ass-whooping but she couldn't touch either one.

As soon as she stepped off the elevator, Star's phone began to ring. Although she had been cursing his name only a few seconds before, her heart leaped to her throat with hope that it was Polo calling. When she saw that it was actually Kevia, her eyes rolled to the back of her head.

"So how was it? He really got a big dick?" Kevia asked before Star even got a chance to say 'hello'.

"Bitch, let me tell you about this long forehead ass ni—"

Star's words faded just as she stepped outside of the glass double doors of the hotel. Her mouth snapped shut as she stared in front of her.

"Huh? Star, what did his ass do? You know, I really ain't never liked his ass anyways with them sneaky ass eyes. You don't even need his—"

"Kevia, let me call you back!" She hung up the phone before Kevia even got a chance to finish and stuffed her cell phone in her clutch, fastening it before looking back up... right into his eyes.

"You were about to leave without saying shit to me?" Polo asked, eyeing Star suspiciously, as if she was the one in the wrong.

"Me?" She pressed her hand flat against her chest. "You weren't even here! How am I the one leaving without sayin' shit? Now you better tell me where you were!"

Silence passed between them. Polo's eyes almost felt like they were cutting through her, but Star held her ground. She wasn't a coward, and she needed him to see that. He wasn't about to play her like any other female, because she *wasn't* just any other female. It didn't matter who he was; she would bow to his power in the streets, but she wasn't about to lay down and take his blatant disrespect.

Polo regarded her with curiosity and awe, but his expression didn't let on his inner thoughts. Deep down, he knew he had been too mannish with her the night before, but he hadn't been able to help it. It was how he was used to doing things. Never before had he been worried about another woman's pleasure over his until it came to Star. He knew she was different; she wasn't one of those women he could mutt, and he really didn't want to, but he couldn't escape the nagging feeling that she still couldn't be trusted.

Even though he had conquered so many things, never in life had he mastered how to control his anger. The only way he knew how to channel his aggression was by force; by making himself superior and pushing everyone else beneath his feet. Star, no matter how much a jewel he knew her to be, would eventually meet the same fate. And it wasn't even that he wanted to harm her on purpose. Simply put, she was just mixed up with the wrong nigga at the worst of times and in the midst of the most unfortunate circumstances. He didn't want to break her down, but he wasn't equipped with what it took to build up a woman of her caliber and make her better.

"Let me hold your hand," he said, his tone much gentler than it had ever been before.

Squinting up at him, Star felt her fire begin to subside. It was like he was opening a padlocked door and giving her a look into his soul. His eyes were soft, and he seemed unsure of himself, nervous even. Feeling the warm, fuzzy feeling she hadn't felt since the night before, Star reached out and placed her hand into his.

"I told you that you are mine because I'm feelin' you. No other chick can say that she belongs to me right now but you. You gotta believe that. It's real shit."

Star was ready to eat out of the palm of his hand. But then his eyes went dark, and the tension returned to his face. It was like catching a glimpse of Bruce Banner turning into the Incredible Hulk. Even his touch seemed to go from fire to cold as ice.

"But let me get this straight. Questionin' me 'bout the shit I do is the quickest way to change that. And you better not leave without tellin' me where you're going. It's for safety reasons," he added. A bold-faced lie. "Remember that so you don't do this shit again."

Star snapped her neck back and was about to tear right into him, but one long stare down stole the breath from her body. He was making things crystal clear. She was his, but *he wasn't hers*. Just because she'd given him rights to her body didn't mean the same rules applied when it came to his. It wasn't a concept that she could quite compre-hend, so she did something that she would grow more accustomed to doing in the months that followed: closed her mouth and simply nodded her head.

CHAPTER 13

"What kind of hair you got?" Star asked, hands on her hips as she looked at her new client.

Although she needed the money, she was not enthused about tending to this client on this day. Roxy's nosy, fiending ass had been trying to find out for weeks now where Star was stashing her money. Roxy blamed her for turning in the drugs and money to Polo, convincing him that Steve had stolen it himself and was trying to get them to hide it before he was killed. Although it had to be done to cover their own asses, Roxy felt like Star owed her something for it.

Nearly every day, she saw the clients that Star had coming through and was convinced she was racking up major money and refusing to break bread. To avoid drama, Star would schedule her clients early in the morning when junkies like Roxy were fast asleep after spending the entire night getting high. But her mama smelled money coming a mile away, and for that exact reason, this time, she was up and walking about when Star's client arrived.

"I bought the Marley hair," the girl replied, shrugging her shoulders.

Grabbing up one of the hair packs, Star opened it and fingered the hair.

"This might be alright," she replied and then sighed before grabbing a comb and sectioning off her head.

"Do we gotta sit out here in the sun?" the girl whined, and Star rolled her eyes. To be damn near as old as she was, she acted like a big kid.

This bitch got a big ass head, she thought, lightly sucking her teeth.

Two hours later, Star was nearly done when Roxy finally sashayed her ass out the door, hands on her hips, head cocked to the side, and lips poked out as she eyed the faux locs that she was installing.

"Damn, girl. That style right there is *everything!* Star, you gon' do me next?" she asked, smirking as she asked the question, her eyes still on Star's client.

Picking up on the game that Roxy was playing, Star didn't even bother answering her. Roxy knew damn well she didn't sit still long enough to get anything done to her head. Not to mention, her edges had been snatched from her scalp a long time ago. There was nearly nothing left to grip to begin with, which was why Roxy stayed sporting old wigs and full weaves.

"It looks good for real?" the girl asked, smiling hard as Roxy nodded her head in affirmation. "I can't wait to see it. I been wanting this style done for a minute but ain't found too many people that can do it right."

Rolling her eyes, Star grunted, wishing that the girl would just shut up so that Roxy would go away. She was always inserting her ass in someone's else business instead of getting into some of her own, and that was the main reason why Star couldn't wait until graduation day. Once she walked across that stage, she was unstoppable. She could leave and live without worrying about her thieving ass mama stealing everything that she was working hard for.

"Well, my baby is hookin' your ass up for real, so you ain't gotta worry 'bout what them other bitches can't do. Plus, they be chargin' a grip for a style like this! I know Star gave you a discount, didn't she? How much she charged you?"

The girl's eyes widened, and she started nodding, licking her lips before answering Roxy's question.

"You right, because one chick was gon' charge me $280, but Star only charges—"

"That ain't none of her business what I do and don't charge!" Star snapped, cutting her off before she could finish.

But it was too late. Roxy was already leaning on the back of her heels with her arms crossed in front of her chest and a satisfied smirk glued to her face. Although Star had been claiming that she was doing hair and makeup for the experience and wasn't making anything from it, Roxy's conniving ways had confirmed what she'd already thought. Not only was Star charging, but she was probably making big money off of it too.

"I knew your ass was out here rackin' up but don't wanna give nobody no money for food, rent, or shit. Greedy bitch." Roxy sneered, cutting her eyes at her daughter.

It didn't matter that Roxy didn't bring in any money to cover rent, food, or anything else either. It also didn't matter that Star hadn't asked her for a single dollar since the day she realized how she could make money for herself. In Roxy's mind, Star was her daughter, and that fact alone meant that she was owed a piece of anything that she brought in. And when she got it, the last thing that money would go to was food and rent. Roxy would smoke up all of Star's earnings into a black smog before the week's end.

"I'm sorry..." the girl muttered as soon as Roxy had walked back into the house, but not without shooting Star a long, disapproving stank ass glare. Star knew that she was only walking inside to tear up the house, looking for her stash once again, but she was certain that Roxy would never find it. At least that's what she prayed.

"It's okay," Star replied in a sad tone. "You didn't know no better."

Although she already knew the type of person Roxy was and she'd been that way for as long as she could remember, it still hurt to have a mother who didn't give a damn about her. That was one thing that a person could never get used to no matter how they were brought up. Any child brought into the world was owed love by their parents—a mother at the very least. Star was robbed of that from day one. There had never been a time where she sincerely felt the comfort of a mother's love. It was damaging to the development of a child and left irreparable scars that Star didn't even know she had.

The block got live, and in only a few moments, the stinging pain from her exchange with Roxy was just another bad memory that she would reflect on later. The sun rose to its highest point in the sky, enveloping the Chicago hood in its warmth. Days like this when it was the hottest, crime was the highest. There was something about the heat that made niggas less tolerable, ready to pop off at the drop of a dime. Black folks hated the cold so that was when shit slowed down, but the heat brought out the savages, and this day was definitely one of the hottest.

"You almost done?" the girl whined, fanning herself with her hand. "It's hot as hell out here."

Sighing, Star wiped the sweat off her brow with one hand. They were in the shade, but it wasn't making any difference. She was smoldering, nearly melting, but even that was more tolerable than going inside and dealing with Roxy and her attitude.

"I only got like ten more, and then you'll be finished."

"Thank God!"

Placing the next piece of hair in her mouth, Star held it as she made her next part, but some commotion from across the street grabbed her attention. Looking up, she saw a group of niggas standing outside of the Disciple's trap house... and Polo was right in the middle.

Over the past few days, she hadn't seen him, but he'd been texting and calling her every chance he got, letting her know that he hadn't forgotten about her. She learned what it meant to be with a man of his caliber. He was heavy in the streets, and that meant he couldn't be as accessible as she wanted him to be. She told herself that there was nothing wrong with that because while he got shit done, she got shit done too. But when he called or texted her, she dropped everything she had going on in order to speak to him.

"You went to the prom with Polo, didn't you?" the girl asked, making a smirk rise up on Star's lips as she thought back to the last weekend.

"Yeah, he took me," she replied.

"That mean y'all go together?"

Rolling her eyes, Star thought about telling the girl to mind her own business, but she couldn't resist letting it be known that it was true. They did go together, and she was now Polo's girl.

"Yeah, that's what that mean."

"But I thought he was with Tonya."

Sucking her teeth, Star placed her hands on her hips and then frowned into the girl's eyes.

"You want me to finish your hair, or you wanna play Question Lady for the day? Stop with all that shit, a'ight?"

The girl twisted up her lips and cut her eyes away. "I was just askin'," she said in a low tone.

"And I was just tellin'," Star snapped, picking up her phone just as it had started to ring. It was Kevia. Normally, she wouldn't have even answered the call while doing hair out of respect for her client, but since she was aggravated, she didn't mind making her wait.

"Hold on a minute. I gotta answer this," she said, ignoring the girl when she sucked her teeth and gave her a dirty look.

Placing the phone to her ear, Star sat down on the opposite end of the front stoop with her eyes still on Polo. He was fresh to death, casually dressed in a simple Gucci t-shirt with matching sweatpants, the obvious standout in a crowd of niggas who could only wish they were just as fly. Standing in the center, he was talking to his team as they all listened intently, focusing on his every word. Somewhere in the middle of what he was saying, he found time to cut his eyes to Star, and a subtle smile passed across his lips. It was gone in the next second, but she'd caught it anyways. The butterflies in her stomach came alive, fluttering so viciously that her stomach began to churn.

"Star! Are you there?"

The urgency in Kevia's tone brought her back down to Earth, and she frowned.

"I'm here? What's up, girl? You sound like—"

"Bitch, listen! My cousin's friend who own that hair salon downtown just said that her client just heard from her half-sister's cousin that stays next to Brenda that Tonya and them bitches are comin' over there to jump you!"

Screwing up her face, Star repeated Kevia's words in her mind slowly, not totally following her.

"Wait, you said that your cousin's friend's client's half-sister—"

"Star, forget all that shit!" Kevia interrupted, sounding winded as if she was running somewhere. "That bitch and her pigeon squad are comin' to your spot to jump you! You need to watch your fuckin' back. They said Tonya wanna give you a violation for some shit, but we both know that hatin' ass bitch is just jealous because of you and Polo. I'm at the clinic with my little sister, and that's the only reason I'm not there right now, but I'm on my way just—"

As Kevia continued speaking, Star zoned out, realizing exactly what she was saying. As head of the Gangstress, Tonya could find any reason to order Star to be violated, and it would be vicious. Definitely much worse than what she'd gone through in order to get jumped in. Niggas died during violations, and the worst part of it was that you weren't allowed to fight back. If violated, you had to just take that shit and hope that you'd live to see another day.

But Star wasn't going out like that.

Shit! she thought, hearing her own heartbeat thumping in her ears.

"I gotta go right now. Call me when you're close," Star said to Kevia and then hung up the phone.

She placed the cell phone down and then pressed her hands to the side of her head, trying to get her thoughts together, but she was in a state of panic. There was no telling when Tonya would make her move, and she had to be ready. Glancing back across the street, she looked over to Polo, thinking about running over to tell him what was going on, but he was gone just that quickly. She was all alone.

Snatching her phone back up, she scrolled to his number and pressed the number to call him. With tears in her eyes, she waited for the call to connect, but her heart dropped when the phone went straight to voicemail. Even with Tonya at the head of the Gangstress, she would have had to get all violations approved by Polo first. Did he approve this one?

"Um... is everything okay? I mean, I see you got some personal shit goin' on, but I ain't tryin' to be here all day," the girl she'd been working on said, pushing her big, bubbly lips out as she gave Star major attitude.

"Listen, you gotta go," Star told her, rushing around to collect her things. She grabbed the half-used pack of hair that was left, her purse, and her unopened packs before forcing them into her lap.

"What!" The girl frowned, looking from the packs of hair on her lap to the distressed expression on Star's face. "Hell naw! I paid you to do my hair and—"

"You need to get the fuck out of here now!" Star cut in, speaking forcefully through her teeth. "Some shit is about to go down. A group of Gangstress are on their way over here now, and you don't want to be here when it happens."

With eyes wide, the girl froze as if she didn't fully understand what Star was saying, but when she saw her bend down to remove a loose brick and remove a small pistol, she jumped up, feeling the full weight of Star's words.

"Shit! Girl, I'll holla at you later!" She took off down the block, and in less than thirty seconds, she was gone.

Pushing the gun into the back of her jeans, Star searched for another loose brick where she kept a case of bullets. She hated guns, hated to even feel like she needed one, but she had no choice. Where she grew up, she learned a lesson about how to never be caught without one or lackin', as they called it in the streets. The moment you did could quickly turn into your last moment. For that reason, she stashed a gun in her room, but she also made sure to hide one outside in case anything popped off and she had to make a fast move. Too often, things took a quick, deadly turn, and she was determined not to be a casualty unless she couldn't help it.

And this was one of those cases.

She heard the sound of shuffling feet much too late. Concentrating too hard on loading her pistol, she'd done the one thing she told herself never to do: she got caught slipping.

Whap!

Star didn't even have a chance to react. A sharp, heavy object, probably the same brick that she'd removed a few seconds earlier, smashed against the side of her head, and she blacked out for a brief moment.

When she came to, her face was planted on the cement, and she felt a wet, sticky substance oozing down from her hairline. It was blood.

"Tag. You're it, bitch."

Even though she couldn't see through the stars in her eyes to make out a face, she recognized the voice immediately. It was that bitch Tonya. Mentally, she urged herself to fight, but her body wouldn't cooperate. It was like she was paralyzed; she couldn't move a muscle.

Her fear was palpable, and Tonya could feel it. Looking down at Star, she was energized by her hate for the girl. How dare Polo toss her to the side like used garbage for this weak ass bitch? She was better than Star in every way; her body was tighter, she was prettier, she was more vicious, and then on top of all that, she was a *boss bitch*. Only the queen of the Gangstress had what it took to ride next to the king of the Gangstas, and that was what she was. If Polo couldn't see that she was the woman for him, she would make it so that he had no other choice and extinguish any bitch that threatened her spot, Star being the first one on the list.

"Put her ass in the trunk," she ordered Brenda who was oddly quiet. Brenda hesitated, and Tonya gave her a hard look to let her know that she didn't plan on repeating herself.

"Okay," Brenda replied in a hushed tone and pointed at three other girls to help her out.

With her arms folded in front of her chest, Tonya wore a shit-eating grin and watched as they lifted Star's limp body up, grunting and all as they completed the task. She wasn't about to get her hands dirty right now because she was saving all that for later. Star was about to get violated, and she planned to personally handle her punishment, something she never did, but that was how much she despised her.

Like Star, Polo was Tonya's first. Many years ago, she was just like Star, a little girl growing up in the hood who kept to herself and minded her own business. The only difference between her and Star was that Tonya was eager to get loose. Raised by her grandmother who was deeply religious, she kept close reigns on Tonya and wouldn't let her do shit unless it had to do with the church.

At fifteen years old, she was a virgin, but it was not by choice because her pussy had been hot for niggas since she'd caught the pastor getting his dick sucked by the church secretary years before. It was then that she realized that it all was part of a con. The same nigga who was in church every Sunday jumping up and down, working up a sweat, talking about how the fire of hell was going to come down and burn up all the sinners, was the biggest sinner of them all. He was fuckin' half the chicks in the church, using the same mouth he kissed his wife with to suck on his secretary's big ole titties.

From that day on, she played the part of a good little girl and did everything her grandmother told her, but she knew better and couldn't wait until she graduated and moved away so she could do her own thing. Freedom came faster than she thought when her grandmother died on her fifteenth birthday. She was distraught and lost with no one to turn to.

The same church that her grandmother had dedicated her life to, faithfully paid her tithes and offerings to, and worked hard to build up, wouldn't even fork over the money to bury her. Devastated and with nothing to her name, Tonya felt so alone, but then Polo came to save the day. Without even waiting to be asked, he dropped stacks on her grandmother's funeral and told her that he would step up to take care of her. All he needed was her loyalty. She gave him all that and more.

For the next nine years, she was by his side, helping him build his empire, being the support he needed in order to get to the top. He was her first, and he was her only. She vowed to never in life give herself to another man, even though the only thing Polo was faithful about was constantly sticking his dick in other women. Still, Tonya didn't bitch about it, because he didn't give any of them what he gave her. She was the queen, the head of the Black Gangstress, and the only woman he officially claimed as his own.

That is... until Star came along.

Truthfully, Tonya sincerely felt like Star knew more about Mink's death than she let on. A woman knew another woman, and she was certain that Star was hiding something, but that fact wasn't the only thing that fueled her hate. For some time now, she'd picked up on how fascinated Polo was by her. From forcing her to be made a Gangstress, to personally requesting her presence in the trap house, he was a little too interested in her for Tonya's comfort. But when he easily let Star slide the night of Mink's murder, it became too much for her to hold inside.

After years of never questioning his decisions, never going against him, and always following his demands no matter how much she disagreed, she finally spoke up and told him how she felt about Star. She demanded that he get rid of her—kill her in retribution for Mink's life. She told him that he had to choose; it was either her or Star. After the years they'd spent together, she knew there was no way Polo would turn against her.

But things didn't go as she planned. Polo refused to bend to the commands of a woman, and in less than an hour, he'd kicked her out of the home they'd shared, giving her nothing but the clothes that she wore on her back. She was devastated and once again, alone. But she still had her crown; she was still the head of the Black Gangstress. At least he hadn't taken that, even though he'd taken everything else. Now it was the only thing she had left.

CHAPTER 14

STAR WOKE UP IN A PANIC, GASPING FOR AIR AND SCARED FOR HER life. Somewhere between being tossed in the trunk by a group of Gangstress and this present moment, she'd gone unconscious and woke up only after being doused with what felt like a bucket of water. She was blindfolded and couldn't see a thing, which made her fear even greater. To awake to darkness and not have even the slightest idea about where you were and what was about to happen was a dreadful thing. She could have been sitting on the edge of a cliff, ready to topple to her death if she made the slightest movement for as much as she knew.

An evil cackle of laughter rang in her ears, and she felt her heart nearly leap to her throat. She preened her ears and tried to pick up on even the smallest sound, any hint as to where she was and who all was around her. Tonya's laughter echoed around her like she was in a tunnel or maybe an empty room, but that was it. She had no other clue about her location, but she knew that whatever was about to happen wouldn't be good. When it came to torture, she'd learned through rumors and also seen with her own eyes that Tonya's creativity was endless in that area. It was like she spent night after night trying to come up with some new shit she could use on the next bitch to cross her. And Star was convinced that she'd never hated anyone the way that she hated her. That meant that whatever she had planned would most likely be the most horrific punishment her cruel mind could imagine.

"Take the blindfold off," Tonya hissed, and Star shuddered; the sight of it made Tonya laugh even more.

She had Star right where she wanted her. She was vulnerable... helpless. There was no one to save her.

Star felt hands on her as someone roughly tugged at the blindfold, pulling it from her eyes. She began to struggle but could barely move. She was strapped to a chair; her ankles and wrists were bound by rope tied so tightly that it cut through her skin.

Blinking, Star relaxed only slightly when she realized that she was in the Gangstress' den. It was familiar territory, though that didn't really mean shit. The same place that she knew as the den was about to become her grave once Tonya was through.

"I don't know about this," someone said.

The voice was shaky, nervous. Star craned her neck around and saw that it had come from Sheena, Brenda's homegirl, who had been caught by the police and charged with jumping Star but freed when she refused to press charges.

Biting down on the corner of her lip and scrolling her eyes from Tonya over to Star, Sheena shuffled her feet after speaking up. She didn't want to have anything to do with Tonya's plan. For one, Polo didn't order this violation and knew nothing about it, but that wasn't just it—she liked Star.

Star was a thorough chick. She had the opportunity to turn rat, but she didn't do it. In Sheena's mind, that meant that she owed Star one. They weren't friends, but they were both Gangstress, and Star had proven her loyalty. Sheena didn't want anything to do with punishing her when she knew the real reason behind it was some personal shit that Tonya had going on.

"Do you think I fuckin' care what you think, Sheena?" Tonya snapped, gritting with her nose high in the air. Sheena's eyes snapped to her leader, and she took a few paces back, shrinking under Tonya's malicious stare.

"No, but I—uh, it's just that Polo didn't order this and—"

"Bitch, shut up, or your ass gonna be next!" Tonya shouted, trying to quiet Sheena before she got the chance to finish her sentence. It was too late. Star heard it, and the words sent a jolt of energy through her body.

Polo didn't order this, she thought. *That means I can fight back.*

What Tonya was doing was wrong, and that was everything that Star needed to know. If she could get out of this and let Polo know that Tonya had went rogue, enforcing some shit that she didn't even have the power to do, it would be Tonya that would be catching the violation instead.

Biting down on her bottom lip, Star began to struggle against the rope on her wrists, trying to free herself without Tonya picking up on it. Her gun was gone, but she had her fists if nothing else and they had gotten her out of plenty of shit many times before. With nothing to lose, she would bank on herself to get out of this one since she had no one else to turn to.

"What the fuck am I gettin' violated for?" Star asked with a thick tone, trying to buy herself some time. "I ain't done nothin'."

Tonya's eyes fell on her, and the glare in them was so intense that it was like rays of fire shooting out like lasers. Star was more afraid than she'd ever been in her life, but you couldn't tell it from looking at her. She sat stoic, appeared unfazed, sitting tall with her nose in the air and a vicious scowl on her face as she awaited whatever was coming next. The only thing that was keeping her together was that she knew showing fear would only add fuel to Tonya's fire.

In the hood, people preyed upon fear. Keeping it gangsta in the deadliest circumstances was a defense mechanism because only the strong survived and being weak made you a casualty. From the outside looking in, people thought that the hood birthed killers, but that wasn't how it really was. The hood birthed *survivors.*

"Bitch, you a fuckin' liar," Tonya started, narrowing her eyes.

Star watched in silence as the gang queen pulled out her custom-made brass knuckles from her pocket and placed them on her fingers, flexing as she adjusted the fit. Plenty of times Star had witnessed Tonya pulverize chicks with them. The brass knuckles were actually made from real gold with diamonds embedded in them. They were pretty, glamorous, and deadly. One good hit with them was enough to send a bitch to her knees, and Star had seen it done a few times before while standing next to Kevia, watching and praying that she would never be on the receiving end of them.

But here she was.

"You might have fooled Polo, but I know better. You know more about what happened to Mink than you're lettin' on, and I'm about to get to the bottom of it."

Screwing up her face, Star could barely believe what she was hearing. Tonya was *still* on this bullshit? After all this time, she couldn't find something better to pretend to be mad about? It was no secret that her real beef was the fact that she'd heard all about the fact that Star was the one riding shotgun in the whip while Polo drove her to prom and that they'd spent that night together, but the least she could have done was come up with something better to violate her for other than what went down with Mink. When he was alive, Mink didn't even like Tonya, and they were always bumping heads. She didn't give two shits about the fact that he was dead, and the whole hood knew it.

Moving slowly as she walked up on Star like a lioness stalking her prey, Tonya's lips pulled back into a tight sneer. She balled her fists up, enclosing her fingers around the brass knuckles, and then brought her hand back, gearing up for the first hit. Star gritted her teeth and bared down as she braced herself to take it. Her hope was that Tonya would hit her so hard that she would black out and wouldn't have to endure the remainder of the torture.

"Wait, Tee," Brenda said, interrupting Tonya just before she could get her first lick in. "Why don't you let her loose? Make this shit interesting for us."

Both Star and Tonya wore similar frowns on their faces as they each turned to look at Brenda. Star's upper lip twisted up in disgust as she looked at Brenda's nasty ass grin. To think that Star had actually spared her and didn't turn her into the police just for her to do some sleazy shit like this.

What Star didn't know was that Brenda was actually trying to help her. Although her loyalty was to her friend, Brenda couldn't help the fact that she too had developed a liking for Star. The girl had heart, if nothing else. It was hard to not like somebody who had so much gangsta when you grew up being taught to admire that trait in others. She couldn't sit still and allow Star to be crushed by Tonya without the chance to at least defend herself, and she knew that Tonya's ego wouldn't allow her to back down from a challenge.

"What the fuck you mean 'make this interesting for us'? I don't give a fuck about what y'all find interesting. This is about a violation and nothing else!" Tonya barked out her lie as if everyone else in the room didn't already know the truth.

Taking a deep breath, Brenda stepped forward to answer her, wringing her hands in front of her as she spoke.

"I mean, just keep this shit gangsta. Let this go down like it did in the old days... Y'all go toe-to-toe and let her give it the best she got. We all know that you gon' squash this bitch, but this way, she can't lie and say it wasn't a fair fight," Brenda explained with a shrug. "We already know how slimy this bitch moves. She'll go to Polo the first chance she gets, runnin' her mouth about how she wasn't given a fair chance. I mean..." She licked her ashy lips, shrugging once more. "You could just kill her, and you wouldn't have to worry about her at all, but then you'd have to explain to Polo how a Gangstress was killed on your watch and without his command. I know you don't want that heat on your head."

Nodding, Tonya let her mind meditate on Brenda's words, soaking it all in. She was right. Killing Star would be a quick and easy solution to get rid of her for good, but then she'd have to deal with Polo's wrath afterward. Based on how he'd reacted before when it came to Star, that wasn't the smart thing to do. Brenda's plan was much better; she'd be able to put Star in her place, deliver the message that she was not to be fucked with, and keep Polo's fury at bay.

"Untie her," Tonya ordered, and Brenda wasted no time moving to do as she was asked.

"Thank me later," Brenda whispered in Star's ear as she released the ropes from around her wrists. It was then that Star realized that she was actually being a friend and not a foe. Turning, she watched Brenda with gracious eyes, thankful for the mercy she was given.

Tonya handed her pink chrome pistol to Brenda and Star felt her heart thump with relief. Still, her entire body radiated pain, but she tried not to dwell on it.

Damn, I do not want to fight this crazy bitch, she thought to herself as she looked at Tonya's lean, athletic figure.

One look at Tonya's Instagram let you know this wouldn't be an easy fight. The chick stayed in the gym. She was agile, strong, and ran five miles on the treadmill every day. Her cardio was on point. The last time Star had run anywhere was over a year ago, and that was only because her neighbor's monster pit bull had gotten loose and chased her around the block three times before he was caught. Star had courage, but what use was that when there was a good chance you would still get your ass beat?

With hubris, Tonya stroll over to Star like she was on a stage. The long ponytail atop her shaved head cascaded down her left shoulder as she wiggled her fingers, allowing her blue aqua-green long fingernails to shimmer in the lucid lights like feminine talons.

"Bitch, I'ma give you a head up fade. A fair fight with just me and you one-on-one 'cause your fat ass been needing another trip to the hospital... maybe even the morgue. Now get the fuck up," Tonya spat as she took several steps closer, preparing for battle.

"You gon' give me a fair fight..." Star repeated, doubtfully, while getting her wits together. It was a tactic to prolong time.

"Bitch, just get yo' fat, bad body ass up," Tonya snorted and was rewarded with a litany of laughter and a few snide remarks.

"Bogus bitches," Star mumbled under her breath, annoyed at Tonya and her gang of birdbrain followers.

She had already decided on a tactic for fighting back—the same one she'd used many times in school on other chicks who had tried to jump her. She was going to be a human windmill of feet and fist in one violent tornado of torrential blows, all aimed at Tonya. Star had once fought two girls in high school like that and won, knocking one of the girls out cold inside the same locker room they'd tried to jump her in.

The only problem was, Tonya wasn't a girl in high school. She was a whole, grown ass woman, mean as a Pitbull and known best lately for fighting even big ass men with that infamous ponytail swinging in the wind as if it was the source of her strength.

As Star was about to get up out her seat, Tonya violently kicked her in her chest. Just as the old rickety chair was toppling over backwards, she heard a loud whooshing sound that hissed. It was the air expelling from her lungs like a balloon with a hole in it. As Tonya quickly delivered another punishing blow with the brass knuckles striking Star square in her face, she tried to throw another punch and missed, making the brass knuckles dislodge from her hand and fly across the room.

Star hit the concrete head first with a loud thump and at the same time something metal flew across the floor. It was the gun that she had concealed in the spine of her back. In all the commotion and her near unconscious state of mind, she had forgotten all about it.

Tonya looked over at the small hand gun and chuckled at Star's expense.

"This stupid hoe got a burner on her. Now the ass whooping finna get that much worse, bitch!" she huffed with malice as she replaced the bloodied metal knuckles back on her hand.

Wham! Wham! Wham!

The assault was vicious. She punched Star in her face with the heel of her hand, determined not to destroy her fingernails. The entire time, even though Star was nearly powerless to fight back, she somehow managed to ball up in a fetal position to protect herself as she writhed in agony.

Tonya continued to wail on her with blows to her face so she squirmed over onto her stomach. Tonya was unmerciful in her attack. There wasn't a single doubt in Star's mind about her intentions to kill her. Hatred and jealousy were powerful emotions, egging the fearless head Gangstress to annihilate a girl who didn't even deserve such a brutal beating.

"Now bitch, let's talk. You wanna fuck my man, huh? You wanna be me? Never that... bitch!"

Tonya continued to punish Star as she spoke without pausing long enough to give her any leverage. It wasn't a fair fight at all—she had a weapon. Being hit with brass knuckles was the equivalent to being slugged with bricks. Tonya wasn't giving her a chance to protect herself.

Suddenly Star began to scream, and it was a blood-curdling scream that caught everybody off-guard, including her attacker. In that brief moment, Tonya paused to admire the work she'd put in on Star's face.

Then the unfathomable happened.

Taking advantage of her hesitation, Star began to rise like a Sphinx. In the throes of her painful struggle, she had flashbacks of her grandmother and refused to submit to the death beckoning woes in the back of her mind. Even after enduring Tonya on her back pounding and wailing away viciously on her face, she felt empowered to at least make an attempt to fight back.

The Gangstress in the dank, dingy confines looked on in awe at Star with her face marred with blood and white concrete debris, looking like a possessed zombie as she began to thwart and thrash, tousling with Tonya as best as she could.

"That bitch is crazy!" someone chimed in, befuddled, as Star staggered around with Tonya on her back.

"You... said a... fair fight, you fake ass bitch." Star gurgled her words like she was drunk as blood spewed from her mouth and nose.

By then, even Tonya was shocked by Star's resilience as much as she hated to admit. Out of sheer desperation and determination, she glanced at the gun on the concrete situated next to an iron steel heater. It was Star's gun. Nearly out of breath and winded, it dawned on her that she was going to have to shoot Star and just get it over with if she wanted to maintain the upper hand.

Suddenly, Tonya pushed off Star and backed away. She needed room —she was running out two vital things: her breath and energy.

Fightin' this fat ass bitch ain't gon' be as easy as I thought, she thought to herself, glancing around at the crowd around her. The awe in their eyes as they looked at Star infuriated her. Once again, her ass was stealing the limelight.

"Fuck all this playin' around. I need to get to the bottom of this shit," Tonya muttered, preparing to walk over to the gun.

The decision was made. She would kill Star, a single shot to the dome and tell Polo it was self-defense. Her proof being that she killed

Star with her own weapon. None of the Gangstress around would dare to challenge her story or they'd meet the same fate.

Star spewed blood from her lips and wiped the rest from her mouth with her arm, smearing it over her face. She looked like road kill and felt like she'd gotten ran over by a semi, but the anger and the adrenaline pumping through her veins was what fueled her to not back down. Flailing her arms about, she had tried her best to fight Tonya off, but she was no match. She was fighting with her bare fists while Tonya had a weapon to aid in her defense. Every punch that she took felt more like a gunshot. It nearly took the life right out of her.

"God help me," Star whispered pitifully, watching Tonya grab her gun from the concrete floor. This was the end and she couldn't do a thing to stop her pending demise. At least she didn't go out like a chump.

Dropping to her knees, she was just about to do something that she'd never done in life. It was time to wave the white flag and tuck her tail between her legs. There wasn't an ounce of fight left in her body. She fought like a champ, but it was for nothing. It was time to throw in the towel and bow to Tonya who had proven she was in fact the head bitch in charge.

Bam!

A loud sound echoed throughout the room, only making the ringing in Star's head worse than ever. Squeezing her eyes closed, she placed her hands to her ears to block out the noise around her, hoping that it would help to stop the radiating pain shooting through her head.

"What da fuck is goin' on in here?"

Polo?

It couldn't be. She must have imagined it. In her state of deliriousness, she figured she had to be hearing things. But when she lifted her head, there he was... standing only a few yards away from her like the savior she didn't even know she'd needed. Even though Star felt like death was near, seeing Polo was just enough to push her to hold on to the last bits of life that she had left. All eyes turned toward the front door as everyone acknowledged their king standing with his soldier, Sloan, by his side.

"Noooo... Star!"

Running in from behind him was Kevia, and once she saw how badly bruised and bloody her best friend was, she didn't break her speed until she was standing right over her. Reaching down, Kevia pulled her to her feet, baring the full weight of Star's weary body as she helped her up.

"Are you okay?" Kevia whispered with tears in her eyes, holding her by draping one arm over her shoulders. "I told Sloan what happened, and he called Polo. I'm so sorry I didn't make it sooner."

Thankful, Star did her best to smile up at her friend, showing off blood-stained teeth. Kevia shuddered, but she was happy that even though she'd come so late, it appeared to be just in time. Star was alive, and she knew that if Tonya had her way, that wouldn't be so.

"What's goin' on is this bitch attacked me!" Tonya bellowed, standing with one hand on her hip as she pointed a long stiletto finger-nail into Star's direction. "She tried to jump bad, talkin' about she couldn't be touched, and I had to show her who the head bitch was. See, that's what happens when you pay attention to these bird bitches, Polo. That dick be havin' them feelin' bold as fuck."

"Bitch, shut da fuck up!" Polo snapped, his voice much louder than normal.

He wasn't the one to raise his voice, but Tonya was pushing him to the edge. One thing he didn't like was for random muthafuckas to be in his business, and that's exactly what Tonya was up to—putting his business in the streets. He was smart enough to know that she was lying. Whatever was going on here was definitely about him, but it hadn't been started by Star. He knew that sometime soon, Tonya would make this move, but he didn't think she would be stupid enough to pull some shit like this.

"She's lying!" Kevia yelled out, quick to provide Star with the defense that she couldn't give herself. "That bitch had the whole block talkin' about how she planned on jumping on Star, and we all know it ain't got shit to do with any other than the fact that her ass is salty about how—"

Stepping forward, Tonya's face was balled up so tightly that she was almost unrecognizable. She reached out, trying to grab Kevia, but

Sloan made a sudden hand movement to his side where his pistol was stashed that made her freeze in her tracks.

With Tonya as Polo's girl, Sloan would have never even considered raising a gun at her, but she was out of line, meaning she was no longer protected by him. Therefore, like all of the other Gangstress, she had to bow to his leadership.

She gave Sloan an incredulous look before panning her eyes to Polo, not believing that he wouldn't call down his man. But Polo simply stood still, his feet planted firmly in the ground further illustrating that Tonya was dead to him and was stripped of his protection. She was on her own, and with every passing moment, she was realizing that it was a very lonely place to be in.

"You fucked up, Tonya," Sloan said in a low tone. "This wasn't sanctioned by Polo... which means that you're the only one here who is at fault, and for that, you should be punished."

All of the blood drained from Tonya's face, making her cocoa-brown complexion appear nearly as white as a ghost.

"Wh-what are you talkin' about?" she stuttered, looking back and forth between the two men standing before her.

She could barely believe her ears. Punished? She was the queen of the Black Gangstress! How in the world could *she* deserve a violation for punishing a member of her own crew?

Watching the exchange gave Star a surge of strength that she didn't even know she had left in her. This had never happened before, as far as she knew. The leader of the Black Gangstress was about to punished for a violation, and it was because of *her*. Polo was coming to her defense. He was protecting her just like he said he would! But nothing in the world could have prepared her for what came next.

"This can't be true," Tonya cried out, her voice beginning to sound more like a tired whine.

"He's right," Polo said, his eyes as black as coal as he stared back at her.

Although he was only a few inches taller than her, his supreme presence seemed to tower above creating a deadly shadow over her body. It was apparent who really held the power in the room. Tonya had made a mistake in thinking that her past with Polo meant more than it did. He was about to show her that she was just as disposable as anyone else who challenged him.

"Star!"

Hearing her name shoot from his lips made her stand to attention. Blood was dripping from her face, and her body was badly bruised, but she couldn't even feel the pain. Something big was about to happen, and she knew it. Everyone else in the room did as well. The crew of Black Gangstress around them looked on in silence; the room was so quiet that you could probably hear a roach scattering across a blade of wet grass outside.

"Yes?" she replied.

Her voice came out coarse and so quietly that she wondered for a second if she had really said anything or if it had actually been in her mind. But when Polo turned his attention on her and she stared into eyes so cold and black, she felt an icy tingle run down her spine.

This was the soldier that the streets whispered about—the one that niggas were afraid to meet under the wrong circumstances. He was the devil incarnate, walking to and fro, terrorizing the hood by merciless violence and force, and in this moment, she wasn't sure about whether he considered her friend or foe. The look in his eyes told her that the man she'd been boo'd up texting with in the days prior was long gone. He was pure goon, and all she could do was pray to God that whatever fate he had in store for Tonya wouldn't be shared by her.

"Tonya is getting violated," he told her with a steel tone. "And you need to be the one to do it."

Beside her, Kevia sucked in a loud breath as did about half of the other Black Gangstress standing around. With one brow lifted, Sloan shot Polo a sideways look.

The hell is this nigga up to? he thought but didn't say a word.

He'd learned over the years of working with Polo that it wasn't smart to test his gangsta during times like this, or he would be next in line to be reminded of why he was revered as a supreme street king.

"You've got to be kidding!" Tonya scoffed, chuckling nervously as she looked around the room, waiting for someone to speak up on her behalf.

No one said a word; even Brenda cut her eyes away from Tonya and looked away, letting her know that she wouldn't intervene or offer up any assistance. Tears tickled the back of her eyes as she turned back to Polo, ready to beg him for mercy that she knew he'd never give. Her mind was frantic. This *couldn't* be happening.

"Polo," Star started, licking blood from her busted bottom lip. "I-I can't—"

Before she could finish, he stepped forward, hovering his lean, muscular frame over her, silencing her words before she could get them out.

"You can, and you will... or else you'll be next." He spoke the words with malice, letting her know that he meant exactly what he said, and dread fell upon her.

Turning to Tonya, Star leveled her eyes on the woman who had been trying her hardest to kill her only a few moments before. And she would have succeeded had it not been for Sloan and Polo walking into the room. Star wasn't naturally violent, and she wasn't one to act first to hurt anyone, but she was a survivor. Tonya had been trying to end her—steal the very breath from her body, and for what? Only because of her own jealousy.

Thinking on that, Star narrowed her eyes and gritted on her, baring and clenching her teeth. Adrenaline rushed through her veins as she thought back on the past few months and all of the pain and agony she'd endured. She'd gotten her ass beat on multiple occasions, ended up in the hospital, had a gun pulled on her best friend in broad daylight, and had been jumped, tossed in a trunk, and brought here to die. No, she never would have come at Tonya under regular circumstances, but that wasn't what this was. This was a fight for survival, and in the end, she planned on being the last woman standing if it called for that.

"Brenda!" Star called out, her voice loud with newfound strength and authority.

Brenda snapped to attention, and the sight of it further emboldened Star. She pointed at her and Sheena who was standing at Brenda's side.

"You and Sheena hold her down."

Both of their eyes went wide, and Brenda looked as if she would protest, but one look at Star and she knew better. Taking a few timid steps forward, Brenda grabbed onto one of Tonya's arms, and Sheena held the other.

Satisfied that Tonya couldn't move, Star walked over and grabbed Tonya's beautiful brass knuckles from where they were lying on the concrete floor at her feet, still covered in her blood. She stared at them, getting angrier by the second before she pulled them on.

"That's my bitch," Kevia whispered behind her, feeling proud of Star's sudden transformation.

She wasn't the only one. Standing to the side, it was hard for Polo to keep down the sly grin that was curving the edge of his lips as he watched Star do her thing. He knew more about her than even she knew. He knew that she had the heart of a goon; he just had to bring it out of her, and that was exactly what he planned to do. She would be his most prized possession and most vicious soldier once he was through.

Rearing back, Star threw a punch aiming right at Tonya's nose, and when the hit connected, a loud crack echoed through the room. The blow dropped Tonya to her knees, sinking fast like her feet were tied to an anvil. In the background, Brenda let out a shrill scream that sent shivers up Kevia's spine.

Star pulverized Tonya that day. Truth be told, she didn't even need the brass knuckles, and after the first hit that brought Tonya down, she tossed them to the side and began to hit her with her bare fists. She was a monster, brutal to the core and energized by her own pain as she gave Tonya every bit of the same merciless beating that she'd given to her.

By the time Star was finished, Tonya was leaking from her nose and her mouth, spewing blood from her lips as Brenda and Sheena struggled to hold her up. Her legs had turned into jelly, but her eyes still held her rage.

The one thing about Tonya that Polo knew but Star hadn't quite grasped yet was that this wasn't enough to teach her a lesson. Tonya was the type of enemy who would never go away and would spend the rest of her days plotting her revenge. So once Star backed away, Polo moved forward and pulled his pistol out, pressing it right to Tonya's skull as Brenda and Sheena held her arms behind her back.

"Nooo!" Brenda screamed, dropped Tonya's arm, and placed her hands on the sides of her face in agony. "Don't kill her, please!"

Not listening, Polo clenched his jaw and cocked his gun. The sound jarred Star out of her trance. It was then that she felt the need to intervene.

"Polo!"

"Nah, Star. Let him kill that bitch!" Kevia rooted, much less forgiving than Star. A true product of the hood, she understood the same thing that Polo did. When it came to the street life, all enemies had to be extinguished when you had the chance, or you'd spend the rest of your life watching your back.

On the other end, the anger in Tonya's eyes was gone and had been replaced by hurt. She didn't fear death, because she knew it would come at some point. Her first day as a Black Gangstress taught her that. After all, it was how she'd gotten her spot. The reigning queen at the time had been killed by her own hands, and Polo had then given her the throne. Polo had taught her that, in this life, death was the only thing that was promised, but she never ever imagined that she would die at the hands of the only man she loved.

"Baby, please," she cried, allowing tears to run freely down her face. The salt from them burned her bloody wombs. "I thought—I thought you loved me."

She was trying to appeal to a side of him that didn't exist. He had no love in his heart for anyone, not even himself.

"Just let her go," Star pled, her eyes running from Tonya to Polo. As much hatred as she had for Tonya, she couldn't stand by and let the girl be killed. She deserved punishment, and Star had given her that. But this right here was just too much.

Seconds seemed to pass like hours as everyone held their breath in their lungs, wondering and waiting for what would happen next. The air was tense with anxiety, anticipation, and sheer shock of this incredulous situation before them. It was something they'd never fathomed before. The hood's royal couple was no more. The Bonnie and Clyde duo was coming to a tragic end.

And then it happened.

Pulling the gun back, Polo stuck it in the small of his back. Everyone in the room took in a collective breath of relief. This was a day full of miracles. Shit was happening this day that had never happened before, and they could barely believe it. The intensity of the situation was at an all-time high but Polo was full of surprises and he wasn't through. Reaching out to Brenda, he beckoned her to give him Tonya's revolver with the pink handle that she had tucked in the waistband of her jeans... the same one Tonya had shot Kevia with. He then held it out to Star.

"This is yours now. You're the new queen."

Shocked beyond words, Star looked from him down to the gun, not wanting to grab it at first. When he nudged it forward to her once more, she reached out and plucked it carefully from his hand with two fingers like it was hot and would burn her skin.

As soon as she made contact with the metal, a new feeling invaded her. She felt powerful, invincible even. Lifting her head, she looked back at Polo, and the way he stared back at her elevated her to a new level.

"Yeaaah, bitch!" Kevia cheered from behind, and Star felt her lips curve into a small smile.

"Gangstress!" Polo shouted out to the crowd. His deep voice thundered, echoing throughout the room. "Salute your new queen!"

The room exploded around her so loud that Star nearly had to cover her ears. The Gangstress threw their signs up in the air, crowding around her while shouting and celebrating the reign of the new queen. Sloan grabbed Tonya's body up, and she seemed nearly deflated, not at all resisting as he took her out like yesterday's trash. She was the past, and Star was the present and the future.

Jumping up and down, Kevia threw her set up in the air and shouted loudest of them all, making Star laugh. She couldn't believe what was happening. They were celebrating her—hugging her and screaming her name.

Of all the times in her life, this moment felt the closest to what she had always imagined having a family would be life. Finally, at the age of eighteen, she had a crew of women around her rejoicing in her achievements, promising her their loyalty—people who were proud of her and willing to give their lives to save hers, if and when the time came.

"All hail the new queen!" Kevia screamed, starting a chant that the rest of the Gangstress joined in on.

Standing quietly to herself, Brenda wasn't as lively as the rest because Tonya had been her best friend, but after a short while, she came over to Star and held out her hand.

"All hail the new queen," she said to Star, speaking genuinely. "Listen, Tonya is my girl, but I'm a Gangstress before anything else, and the shit she pulled was foul. Feel me?"

Nodding her head, Star slowly reached out to shake her hand. It was then that Star felt Polo's presence beside her. Pivoting on her heels, she looked right into his eyes and nearly swooned when she saw the smirk on his face. He was king, and she was queen; her every dream was coming true.

"Congratulations," he told her, and she simply nodded her head. "After y'all done with all this celebration shit, go home and pack your bags."

Frowning, Star had to blink a few times as she struggled to understand exactly what he was saying.

"Pack? Where am I goin'?"

Clenching his jaw, Polo gave her a look as if he didn't get why she was so confused. As if she was asking why someone needed oxygen to live.

"You're the queen," he said slowly as if speaking to a small child. "So you're coming to live with me. I'll hit you up on your cell when I'm on my way."

And with that, he turned around and walked out of the warehouse, not offering her the opportunity to protest. Even after he'd disappeared on the other side of the door, Star was still standing in the same place, her mind ruminating on what he'd said as the shouting and celebratory jeering continued around her. Someone lit up a blunt and the stench of the smoke burned her nose but still she was frozen in place, thinking on his final words.

Live with him?

It should have been something worthy of its own celebration. For as long as she could remember, she'd wanted nothing more than to leave from out of her grandmother's place, out of the Southside, and be on her own. Living apart from Roxy had been one of her lifelong goals, but now that the time had come, she wasn't sure that she was ready for it. Leaving meant that she would also have to leave her grandmother behind... and she'd have to leave Ebony. What would become of her sister if she wasn't there to protect her?

"Bitch, your *whole life* is about to change!" Kevia exclaimed, clasping her hands together as if in prayer before wrapping her arms around Star's neck and pulling her into a tight hug.

There were tears in her eyes. She was so happy for Star because of all people, she knew her friend's most private dreams. Star wasn't like everyone else... she was so much more. As much of a true friend as Kevia was, she knew that Star's place wasn't in the hood. Star was made to be a *star.* She was supposed to be a leader. She was the one with the potential to make it out of the slums and make something better of herself. And, in Kevia's mind, living big with Polo and running the streets with him as his queen was as good as it could possibly get.

But now that the moment to be great was there, Star wasn't so sure this was what she wanted. All she had dreamed out for herself was to make it out of the hood, get into school, and build a real career for herself. She'd been working her hardest on it, and with her Instagram business booming, she was making her own money and was closer than she had ever been before. But now her life had taken a sudden turn, and she was a key player in some street shit that she had never wanted to even be part of... What would happen to her now?

GANGLAND 2 IS AVAILABLE NOW!

NOTE FROM LEO & PORSCHA

Thank you for reading! We know that we say it every time but this was TRULY a labor of love. We spent a lot of time planning out this series to make sure that we not only stayed true to our characters but true to the story of the gang lifestyle as a whole.

If you're connected with us on our social media pages, you'll know that both of us lived in Chicago for part of our lives and, during that time, we experienced a lot of the circumstances and environments described in this book and the ones to come. It's a tale very close to our hearts and very personal.

Star is a girl like so many others—she's looking for love in all the wrong places. So many women get caught up in this trap and it's hell pulling themselves out of it. We felt compelled to speak on this as well as the issues that have shaped the characters of the ones around her as well. With a mother held victim to her own addictions, Star is left to grow up much too fast and navigate the world alone.

It may be hard not to but don't hate Polo! He's a product of his environment and he was dealt a bad hand, given a rough start at life, and had to do what he felt was required of him in order to make it to the top in the way he was shown by the men in his life before him. Without a proper role model, is it any wonder that he doesn't know how to love? Especially when he doesn't even love himself... this happens every day. You'll learn more about him in the following books and we feel that once you understand him a little better, you may realize that he's a victim of the hood in the same way that Star is— even if he doesn't know it.

In the next book, Kato will make his grand entrance. After all, this series is about the love between Star and Kato. You're probably wondering how that could *ever* work out after getting a glimpse at the type of man he is but life or death situations have a way of changing you in many ways. The hard times show you who is really down for you and who is not and Kato will soon discover this for himself. In everyone, there are redeeming qualities and, though you may not see any of that in Kato just yet... it's coming! Just wait!

Kevia is the best friend that every girl should have. She's loyal, protective and doesn't try to compete against the one she calls her friend. Her story is one many have experienced. Not only is she forced to pretty much raise her brothers and sisters like they're her own children while she is still a child herself but she's insecure and that insecurity leads to her making huge mistakes when it comes to love. Though Sloan may truly love her, she doesn't push him to recognize her worth and eventually, this will lead to some hard consequences that she will have to face alone.

And Tonya... is she really as bad as she seems to be? Or is she a woman who gave her all and everything to the wrong man and allowed him to ruin her? You'll see in the following books that things between her and Polo are far more complicated than what they appear to be. She did what she was supposed to do—gave her loyalty and love to the one person she thought would never betray her because he was the only one there when she needed a helping hand. Now that he's discarded her like trash, shouldn't she be mad?

Leave us a review with your thoughts! We read them and we appreciate them.

Special thanks to our loyal readers, our authors and our core supporters. We appreciate you more than you know.

To all authors out there and especially to the urban community of writers—we find strength when we work in harmony **together**. Spread love, not hate. We are all in this book gang together!

Peace, love & blessings to all,

Porscha & Leo

JOIN THE GANG!

Join the Gangland Series Mailing List

READ MORE ON THE LIT READING APP!

Read more books like this one **for less**! Check out some other new releases on the LiT Reading App. Go to www.litreadingapp.com to learn more!

JOIN THE LSP MAILING LIST!

Join our mailing list to get a notification when Leo Sullivan Presents has another release.

Text LEOSULLIVAN to 22828 to join!

To submit a manuscript for our review, email us.

CPSIA information can be obtained
at www.ICGtesting.com
Printed in the USA
LVHW032115180321
681863LV00006B/1220